THE MAN WHO WAS THERE

B

Also available from the University of Nebraska Press

Wright Morris: Structures and Artifacts
Photographs 1933–1954

THE MAN

WHO WAS THERE

By WRIGHT MORRIS

UNIVERSITY OF NEBRASKA PRESS
LINCOLN   LONDON

COPYRIGHT, 1945, BY
WRIGHT MORRIS

First Bison Book printing: 1977

Most recent printing indicated by first digit below:
1   2   3   4   5   6   7   8   9   10

Library of Congress Cataloging in Publication Data

Morris, Wright, 1910–
    The man who was there.

    Reprint of the ed. published by Scribner, New York.
    I. Title.
PZ3.M8346Man8 [PS3525.07475]   813'.5'2   76–16590
ISBN 0–8032–0881–2
ISBN 0–8032–5813–5 pbk.

The Bison Book edition is reproduced from the first (1945) edition, published
by Charles Scribner's Sons, by arrangement with the author.

Manufactured in the United States of America

CONTENTS

Water seeps downward, fire flickers upward, wood can bend and stretch, metal follows a mould, the earth creates the seedtime and the harvest. By means of that which seeps downward a salty taste is engendered; by means of that which flickers upward, a bitter taste is engendered; through the bending and stretching, a sour taste is engendered; through that which follows a mould, a sharp taste is engendered; through seedtime and harvest, a sweet taste is engendered.

THE GREAT PLAN
THE BOOK OF RECORDS

THE MAN WHO WAS THERE

THE VISION OF PRIVATE REAGAN

IN THE SECOND YEAR OF THE war Miss Elsie Herkimer of Colvin, California, persuaded her mother to leave Omaha and come live with them. This had long been planned, for thirty-five years to be exact, but was made possible through the kindness of Private Christian Reagan. Private Reagan had lived right across the street ever since he was a boy, and Grandmother Herkimer had grown very attached to him. When Christian Reagan joined the army and went off to some camp in California, Grandmother Herkimer went so far as to talk about visiting him. This, of course, was impossible as there was no place for an old lady at an army camp, or off in the desert somewhere. But she agreed to put up with her daughters when it was finally explained that the town of Colvin was near Private Reagan on the map.

This was in the summer of her ninety-second year. As somebody had to ride out with her, and as she insisted on Private Reagan, it was finally arranged that he would bring her back with him on one of his leaves. As Grandmother Herkimer would have nothing to do with loafing in bed while she was traveling, they sat in a coach not far behind the engine and rode west.

There were other problems as well. Grandmother Herkimer would have no traffic with what she found in the ladies' room and insisted on getting off the train whenever it stopped. This was none too often, and between stops Private Reagan had very little peace of mind. In the morning she would wet her lips and her eyes from a paper cup at the drinking fountain, and then block the aisle while she slowly braided her hair. She would glower at people with all of her bone hairpins sticking out of her mouth. But the dining car she thought was wonderful. She answered the first and last call for meals, eating five and six times a day, and Private Reagan did not try to explain it to her. For she was hungry, she was always hungry and ready to eat. There was no explanation for this, but Private Reagan did what he could, sometimes eating as often as four or five times himself. In the morning she would eat from his plate of toast and spear with her fork at his side dish of potatoes, as she was not used to this fancy business of having her own. If a sandwich boy passed through the car, she would have to have something to munch on, and then a bottle of something to wash it down. And when not eating she slept, snoring heavily. Suddenly awakening as if she were pinched, or as if someone had called her name, she would press her nose to the window to look for him. And out of the window she saw just what she knew she would see. What she had seen when she passed this way before. All the way across Nebraska and Wyoming Private Reagan tried to clear this up, but it was no

[4]

use ; Grandmother Herkimer was traveling east. She was crossing the Ohio again, and my, what a time they had had with
that river, the water high and fast, she could tell you ! She was
not awake long enough to burn her eyes on the desert, or to
climb and fall from the mountains, and nothing that she saw
appeared at all strange. She faced it with a quick sudden stare,
as she sometimes looked at Private Reagan—but the light that
entered her eyes illuminated another scene. And there it all
was, just as she had left it, just as she had known. It was a
weird and wonderful voyage, and she sustained it by eating,
incredible eating, as if she were a camel and her memory knew
the long voyage home.

Private Reagan was slow to fathom this. He had returned to
a world that he had hoped would be familiar, only to find that
the most familiar thing in it had left. Left with him, or so it
seemed, but the very next moment had left the world. And on
the third day she abandoned Private Reagan as well.

This occurred sometime during the night, for when she awak-
ened in the morning, she addressed Private Reagan as Agee
Ward. "Agee Ward," she said, "it's time to eat." Now Agee
Ward was a boy who had once lived with Christian Reagan,
twenty years ago, when they were both little boys in the fifth
grade. Grandmother Herkimer had been very fond of him.
But it had been twenty years since Private Reagan had thought
much about him, though he had thought quite a bit at the
time. So had Grandmother Herkimer—and when she called
out Agee Ward's name Private Reagan was sure she had been
dreaming about him. But whether she had dreamed it or not,
Agee Ward he remained. It was Agee Ward's toast she ate at
breakfast, his butter that she tried for lunch, and Agee Ward's

[5]

hat that she wore to keep the sun out of her eyes. Beyond these mountains was Pennsylvania, a town named Paoli, and going there with her was a young fellow named Agee Ward.

Private Reagan said nothing—for what was there to say? It was not too much of a trial as she slept most of the time, but he couldn't help noticing the different way she spoke to him. Her voice dropped, she whispered more, talked about things he didn't understand, and signaled all private matter by lightly squeezing his knee. Private Reagan knew that this was not his leg any more.

At night this gave him a strange feeling and he would frequently go for a drink, or stand in the washroom and look at his face in the mirror. Locked up in the washroom he felt better than he did in the open car, with people who were there—and yet not there, somehow, in their sleep. He passed the night drinking water and thinking about these things.

In the fifth grade Christian Reagan had sat in front of a black boy and behind a white boy who could wiggle his ears. This boy's name had been Agee Ward. He had wiggled his ears during the setting-up exercises and during the *Star-Spangled Banner* whenever they sang. In order to keep his mind on the words Christian Reagan would close his eyes—but during the setting-up exercises this didn't work. He either got dizzy and fell over or got mixed up. He hated this boy so much that he refused to mention his name until he discovered what was wrong with him. Agee Ward was an orphan and what he did couldn't be helped. Because of this Christian brought him home to see his father and mother, so he would know what a father and mother were like. After that things happened so fast that Christian had never caught up with them—and then it was over as suddenly as it had begun. A man with grass stains on his pants knocked on the back door while they were eating breakfast and said he had come for Agee Ward. He said he was Agee Ward's Uncle Kermit and had come for him. Agee Ward had never seen him—only received gold pieces from him—but he had not objected to going away. While Christian and his mother cried in the pantry, Agee Ward got his box of marbles and went out and sat in his uncle's car. His uncle said not to mind about his clothes as they didn't know yet where they were going and until they got there they would be sleeping in the car. Then he gave Christian a five-dollar gold piece and drove away.

Just the week before, Christian's fifth-grade class had had its picture taken—but it was not a good picture of Agee Ward. A girl named Stella Fry had waved her hand right in front of his face. This was because Mrs. Partridge had asked who it was that was chewing licorish tar babies, and Stella Fry had waved her hand in Agee Ward's face to point him out. Out of the corner of his eye Christian Reagan had seen it all happen just as the photographer raised his hand and the shutter clicked. And then Agee Ward had started chewing tar babies again.

Christian bought two of these photographs in order to give one to Mrs. Herkimer, even though Agee Ward's face did not show up very well. So that Mrs. Herkimer would know him, and there would be no doubt in the matter, he wrote Agee Ward's name across the front of his shirt. On his way home from school he had stopped by her house to present it to her.

"I see him," she had said, "always wigglin'."

"That's Stella Fry," he had answered, "that's not his fault."

"That's him," she had said, "that's him wagglin'. Always scrunchin', wagglin', or wigglin' his ears."

"But he's gone," Christian had said. "His uncle came and got him. He's gone!"

"Him gone—?"

"Yes, ma'am—"

"Holy Moses!" she had said. "Holy Mackerel!" This was what Agee Ward always said except when he said *Holy Cow*. "Young man—" she had said.

"Yes, Mrs. Herkimer—?"

"Young man," she had said, "will you stop aping Agee Ward?"

"Yes, ma'am—" he had answered, but when he said that she did a very strange thing. She took his nose between her knuckles and squeezed as if she was pulling it off, and when she had taken her hand away there was his nose. There was her thumb right between her fingers just like his nose.

"Now I've got both your noses," she had said. "Do you like Agee Ward?"

"Yes, ma'am—"

"All right—here's his nose back. Now you've got his nose but see to it you don't get his tongue."

"Yes, Mrs. Herkimer," he had said, just the way Agee Ward would have said it.

"Young man," she had said, "are you sporting with me?"

"No, ma'am."

"Young man, if Agee Ward is gone, you'll just have to be him till he comes back—now do you hear me?"

"Yes, Mrs. Herkimer."

"Holy Moses!" she had said, and took him by the nose and led him out.

That had been twenty years ago and Private Reagan seldom thought about it—nor did he think about it much the following day. Early in the morning he delivered Grandmother Herkimer to her two daughters, neither of whom she recognized. In the confusion he managed to slip away. It was all too complicated to explain, and he also had the feeling that the deception— some kind of deception—would not have occurred except for him. The people who got on at Omaha had simply not got off the train again. Something perfectly solid, familiar, had vanished into thin air, as it neither remained on the train—nor did it get off. He was there and not there—something in the manner of Agee Ward.

During the winter her daughter Elsie called him at Camp several times—once a month, in fact, the first Sunday of each month. But he saw to it that it was impossible for him to get away. Then one night in the spring her boy, Roy, called—and said that she had died.

This was in the spring of her ninety-third year, yet those who knew her were surprised, taken by surprise the afternoon she died. Or rather passed away—as Miss Elsie Herkimer always said.

In the morning Grandma had sat up in bed and called twice for Agee Ward; then in the afternoon, in her sleep, she passed away. To die in your sleep, Aunt Elsie knew, was a special dispensation and not very much like dying after all. She had thought of that while she sat alone, crying, and now she thought of it again while she was phoning Roy. Uncle Roy, Grandma's only boy.

To her friends—that is, everyone that knew her—Miss Elsie Herkimer preferred to be known as Aunt Elsie, and she liked to call them Aunt and Uncle as well. Perhaps this began with calling Mother "Grandma"—and that began when they were just youngsters at home and so long ago there were times that she was really a little mixed up. Sometimes she felt that Aunt Agnes might be right and maybe she was just a little sentimental—but what she *knew* was that she liked people better that way. As she did whenever she wrote someone a letter and called them *Dear*.

When Roy answered the phone she remembered that she should have telegraphed Roy—but she could never spell things right to those people over the phone. Now that there was a war on she wouldn't have phoned for anything else but the passing of Grandma—and as she told Roy first of all, Grandma hardly died. She just passed away, quietly, in her sleep. At first Roy didn't answer and she started to repeat it louder, but right in the middle she could hear him saying, "Yeth, yeth, yeth." This was why they always telegraphed, as when he had to say anything to them it was always very hard to understand. When he was a boy, right before her eyes he had pulled on the white hairs in a mare's tail and the kick had struck him solidly on the jaw. While he talked she could see his face with its twisted comical expression, like the faces men made for babies and little boys. With Mr. Lakeside's memo in her hand she interrupted Roy to say that the funeral was Wednesday, that was tomorrow, and that he should call Private Reagan. As Roy began to speak she remembered to ask about Adelaide—Annie Mae and Adelaide—and Roy said they were just fine. Then, very suddenly, he hung up. There was the operator asking what number she had called and as she never could remember numbers she hung up. While she tried to think what it was the operator rang and gave her the charges. She wrote *$1.35 cents for phone call to Needles,* down on the telephone pad. Then she waited for Aunt Agnes to ask her who it was that just phoned—but Agnes sounded busy so she did something else. Under the telephone charge she wrote: *Charge to Aunt Elsie.* There was no real need to do that since they planned to add everything up and divide it by three, and by everything they meant things like telephone calls. But you can't just stop doing what you've been doing for thirteen years, and would have to start doing again as soon as something like this had passed. On the same pad, at the top, was the word *Grandma,* and beneath it:

> Electric Pad
> Bone hairpins
> Pictures to look at
> Candy?

And now to this list Aunt Elsie added the word—*Flowers*—in her very fine hand.

When Aunt Agnes came into the room with the tablecloth and the silver, in passing Aunt Elsie she reached and touched her hand. She did this without looking, as if she had known just where she would find it, as a Doctor moves down the arm to the pulse. And there it was, picking the white hairs on her chin. Ever since Grandma had come, a year now in April, Aunt Elsie had begun to pick at her chin. Now that Grandma had gone it remained to be seen what she would do.

Through the front porch window Uncle Ben.watched Aunt

Elsie's hand rest in her lap, then, as Agnes left, return to her chin again. At the first step to the porch he stopped and looked at the wisteria, hanging in clusters like grapes, with a crushed fragrance. Every spring he remarked to himself, or to anybody else within hearing, that there was nothing quite like wisteria. Tonight he remarked it again, then, turning to the window, said to himself that Aunt Elsie would be next. He hadn't discussed it with Agnes since she and her sister were the same age and recently Agnes hadn't looked so well. But in his own mind he knew Aunt Elsie would be next. Not that she was delicate, but with her mother gone what was there left a maiden lady could live for? Looking in at her, Uncle Ben was sure he didn't know. When she telephoned to the store he knew that at last Grandma had died, and when he heard her voice he knew she would be next.

He would try to be a little more considerate. As he opened the door he saw Aunt Elsie once more place her hand in her lap, and over it, as if holding a bird, her handkerchief.

"I have just called Uncle Roy," she said.

Uncle Ben crossed the room to the sideboard, where he took off his hat, removed the dip in the brim, then placed it in the bowl.

"He can come all right?"

From the kitchen Agnes said, "Don't you worry about Roy."

"He was her only boy," said Aunt Elsie.

"Yes," said Uncle Ben. From his inside pocket he removed his glasses case, then the glasses, blowing on the lenses as he peered at the light.

"In her sleep," said Aunt Elsie. "Just passed away in her sleep."

[12]

"I was just saying," said Aunt Agnes, "that if it comes as easy to me——"

Uncle Ben said, "You called Mary Ann?"

"She hasn't her own phone," said Aunt Agnes. "She has to come to the neighbor's phone."

"It's sixty-five cents and sometimes you don't get her," Aunt Elsie said.

Putting on his glasses Uncle Ben sat down. The rocker he sat in had been moved three or four inches to the right when Aunt Elsie, telephoning, had pushed it with her knees. Before picking up the *Times* Uncle Ben made the adjustment and settled back as his eyes left the room. Early he had found there was nothing to look at in this room. Every two or three years they changed the furniture around and faced other directions, but he still had to sit and look out of the room. Through the window he could see the Ahearns seated at supper with Mrs. Ahearn's broad back poured into the chair.

"Another long day?" said Agnes.

"Hmmm——"

"You are going to have to cut meat?"

On top of the morning *Times* Uncle Ben saw the pamphlet on which was engraved:

ROSE LAWN GARDENS

All the sacred remains in one cherished spot.

Have YOU made YOUR Permanent Arrangements?
ONE CALL COVERS ALL!

Carefully he turned it on its face and picked up the *Times*. He folded it evenly the long way, then folded the front half and brought the two halves together in the back. This he had learned years ago when he worked in the city and had to conserve reading space on the streetcar. Now he had room but he liked to read that way. One thing that annoyed him about books was their stiff, established nature and nothing to fold while he was thinking of something else.

"People got to eat," he said, "and I'm the only man there to cut it."

Aunt Agnes came to the door and looked at him. Looking back at her, Uncle Ben remarked how much of Grandma she had in her; more than Elsie, Beth, or any of the girls. Now that she had her new teeth, even her jaw set like Grandma's—and the left arm, something in the way her left arm hung. As the meat started frying she turned away and he looked at the *Times*.

Turning back to the stove Aunt Agnes tried each of the chops with the fork prongs and arranged them for tenderness in the pan. This arrangement was always left to right—since Grandma had moved in with them and some of the chops troubled Grandma's teeth. Troubled her teeth but not Grandma, until it was observed that the plates in her glass on the sill were missing four molars. They had never been accounted for. When asked, Grandma remembered that they were there in Omaha—where everything was, including most of Grandma. What she had eaten for thirty years, alone with thirteen rooms, nobody knew, for no one had ever found anything to eat in the house. When Aunt Agnes visited Omaha it was always with a supply of food and the conviction that this year would be Grandma's last. Apples shriveled to the size of walnuts could be found sometimes in the drawers, and in the huge coffeepot, buried in the grounds, several spoons. At ninety-two Grandma could not remember when she had been sick. True, her memory had grown short; all of her daughters she had forgotten and refused right to the last to own. As they grew older and like herself, and then to Grandma far older than she was, she settled for her grand-daughters who still seemed to be young.

Aunt Agnes arranged the chops so the fat one would go to Ben. On his spinach she wiped the knife with which she had just cut the butter, and the wafer of butter she slipped in the juice beneath. Now that they had this business there would be no glasses for Ben. He brought the paper so close to his nose it always seemed that he meant to smell it, and she wondered how he managed in the store. Working in a new store where he didn't know just where things were. For the first time in fifteen years there was money, money left over, and now there was *this*. The man had said that the better caskets were from one hundred and eighty dollars up. That meant that if you asked him you would sound like you wanted a worse one and *that* meant that you didn't ask him. So Grandma's casket was the hundred-eighty-dollar better one.

At the door Aunt Elsie said, "Should I set?" When Aunt Agnes turned she first looked at her chin and then at her face as Elsie's hand dropped to her waist. From there her hand made a smooth stroke over her "tummy" as Dr. Griggs referred to it privately. With this gesture she always tipped forward to peer at her skirt, or at her shoes, if they happened to be new. These were new, brand new, and she stood looking at them.

"I think you did very well," said Aunt Agnes.

"Yes, I think so too," Aunt Elsie said. Putting one foot out between them she said, "There was nothing, just nothing else."

"It's just lucky that they're black," said Aunt Agnes.

"Yes, it is," Aunt Elsie said. Reaching the plates from the cupboard, nodding, "It certainly is," she said.

2

When Roy turned from the phone he wiped his face with his hand to where the beard rasped, then he let it fall. Walking down the hall to the light he stood in the doorway blinking, and to his face in the buffet mirror he said, "Well, she's dead."

Turning, Adelaide said, "Who?"

"Grandma," he said, "my mother—who else?"

"Anybody might die," Adelaide began—then turning Annie Mae whom she was undressing, "You might at least pay attention to what you're saying—and where."

Annie Mae didn't seem to have heard. She was considering why, if her legs were now longer as her mother said, she could still reach her toes with the same arms. Annie Mae was twelve, but for four years she had not gone to school because she had been in the second grade three years. Annie Mae did not want to learn anything. She liked very much sitting on little red chairs in a circle or walking in pairs or standing up to sing. But there was less of that in the second grade. Now she reached with her arms and touched her legs that were longer and her toes that were clear at the end of them. She did that for her mother, but her mother did not understand. Her father understood much more, but now he was standing with his mouth open and looking at his teeth in the mirror.

"This afternoon—in her sleep," he said.

"Well," said Adelaide, "that's nice."

"If I live just half as long—" he said.

"You might wait and talk about it later," she said. Over her head Roy looked at Annie Mae and made a face—he twisted his bent face back where it was straight again. As she always did, Annie Mae covered her eyes, not with her fingers but with the heel part of her hands. Her long fingers thrust out from her face like petals from the heart of a flower, and where the flesh spread thin the light came through her hands. Roy wondered again what it was about Annie Mae. Whatever she did with the hands that bothered other people always seemed very beautiful to him. Like using the palm instead of her fingers to cover her eyes.

"If you don't stop that," said Adelaide, "I might as well give up all I've been doing to keep her hands where they belong."

Roy said, "How soon could you get ready?"

"Get ready——?"

"She's my mother," said Roy.

"It's two hundred miles!" said Adelaide.

"The funeral is tomorrow," said Roy. She didn't say anything and he said, "She would have liked to have gone back home."

"To hear you talk," said Adelaide, "you would think there wasn't a war on."

As if to himself Roy said: "Now I got to call Private Reagan. He brought her out, he might like to go. He might know another boy that might want to go."

"Elroy Herkimer! Are you out of your mind? Strangers to your mother's funeral?"

"We got to have four men," said Roy, "in case we got to carry something. If you got to carry something you need at least four men."

"Well," said Adelaide, "you can count me out. If there's going to be strangers you can count me out."

Over her mother's head Annie Mae saw her father walk into the hall and down the linoleum to the telephone stand. She saw him turn on the light and hunt for the telephone book. That made her smile and cover her eyes for she was the one who knew where it was. One at a time her mother took her hands from her face and one at a time forced the fingers closed. She often did this but this time it hurt. At the end of the hall her father blurred, then the white light in the kitchen, the things on the table and her mother's hands. Warm water ran down her face and into her mouth, which was open, pleasant tasting, like what sometimes ran out of her nose. Her mother stood her up to wipe her eyes and then together they went down the hallway where her father turned to make a face at her.

Sometimes Adelaide thought that she didn't know what she would do—but it had been quite a while, and besides that thought didn't lead anywhere. At one time it led to Bowling Green where she taught for twenty-two hundred a year and people said openly that some day she would be principal.

And then she married—for no reason that she had ever been able to discover except that he was the first one to ask her, and she wasn't so young. Then right off the bat the miscarriage and for three years she might have died—perhaps she should have, which she always thought at a time like this. Rather than live in a god-forsaken place like this with a child that refused to learn, refused to speak except for shaking her head yes or no. For all of this there was no reason, since she could speak when she wanted to, talking in her sleep and whenever she thought she was alone. But when she was asked or you wanted an answer, not a word. Nothing but a wriggling of her hands across the top of things or up and down them, or feeling her own face as if she hadn't felt it before. Or the silly grin she always had for her father or strangers sometimes. Everyone said how sweet it was and taken by itself maybe it was, like in a picture a stranger had taken of her. Madeline, he called her, and said she belonged over a church doorway or something like that, a very funny thing to say, once she had reconsidered it. To live alone with a child like that, sometimes right on her heels for hours and days, then suddenly gone— gone right when she wanted her. There was no use calling, nothing to do but stop everything and go look for her, let everything spoil, burn or both as it sometimes did. Even a cow would come sometimes, but not Annie Mae. And when she found her, in the very next breath she might be off again, quiet as a ghost on her narrow brown feet with the long toes. Not to mention how often she was worried about those long toes. She could never bring herself to ask Dr. Finch if there wasn't something hand-like about her feet, for this would be saying there was something monkey-like about her. And the truth was—but never mind, it all meant extra money for shoes and the Lord knows what it would mean later on. That was no worry now with Roy and the Army doing so well, but she couldn't stop an eight-year worry overnight. Any more than she could stop Annie Mae from going off where she *would* go. Out into the shed on hot summer days to sit in the old icebox they had, her knees drawn up to where they pressed right into her eyes. The only reason Adelaide had found her was because of an old hen who always used to lay her eggs in there. Annie Mae had put her out and got in the box herself. Hearing the cackling of the hen Adelaide thought it would be a snake or something and stood with a big stick when she opened the door. And there was Annie Mae as if she were asleep. She was curled up in a tight little ball with her head between her hands like she—well yes, *exactly* like that. Like pictures she had seen of babies—and there was no denying—but it wasn't that so much as how hard it was to get that idea out of your mind. Especially with a girl like Annie Mae. And when you add to that her habit of crawling into every hole she could find, so that selling the icebox for junk didn't do any good. There was always something she could curl up in. She didn't curl up like that in bed unless someone was sleeping with her and that was why she just had to sleep alone. As Adelaide tucked her in she heard Roy come down the hall and then his shadow came in the door.

"Well, it's all set," he said. She said nothing, *nothing,* and kept her back to him. "I knew Private Reagan would want to go and it turns out his sergeant will give us a hand. Nice soundin' boy; boy named Brace, Sergeant Brace."

"You can count me *out*," she said.

"Funerals aren't so long today," said Roy. "I figured some boy would go along just to get a ride to the city, spend a night in the big town." She said nothing and he said, "And I figured while we were at it you might like to get into town yourself. We could stay over and you could have a day to shop."

Adelaide kept her back to him, patted the bed. Naturally she had thought of that—a woman living off here couldn't help but think of it—but she had had the taste, she was thankful, not to mention it. Now that he had—well, she might as well go. She remained stooped over Annie Mae, smoothing the covers and folding her hands until Roy understood what her silence meant. Then he went back down the hall to the bathroom and closed the door.

3

Private First Class Reagan was waiting where he said he would be. As Roy pulled up to the curb he wondered if anybody else might think that Private Reagan looked funny—funny to be seen at a funeral, that is. On the other hand, it was perfectly clear that Private Reagan was a clean-cut boy. He had a very steadfast look that made him seem taller than Roy found him when he got out of the car to shake his hand. As he was wearing pants like everybody, Roy wondered what it was that seemed a little odd about his legs. It was impossible to say except that they seemed as if they were planted and weren't really part of what he was above the waist. But he was a good-looking boy; hard to tell really how old he was, but with a very young look about his mouth. And a very open look about his face. Turning to Adelaide, Roy could see that Private Reagan looked all right, and might even do for a funeral after all.

For Sergeant Brace it seemed they would have to wait. While they were waiting Roy talked about the wonderful Ak-Sar-Ben he had seen in Omaha in 1924. Ak-Sar-Ben spelled Nebraska backwards, and to talk about something like that made people from Omaha feel more at home. Then they talked about where everyone should sit. It would be a pretty long drive, a hundred miles of it right across the desert, so they should sit where they really wanted to sit. It was Roy's opinion that Private Reagan should sit on the shady side because he was new around here and the mountains were wonderful. Private Reagan said he really didn't care. They were still debating this when Adelaide called to them, and there was Sergeant Brace seated in the rear. He was smiling and showing that it was just one of those jokes of his. Looking at Adelaide, Roy could see that Sergeant Brace had a lot to account for, and Private Reagan looked something of the same. His arms were folded, and for a moment Roy was absolutely certain that he would turn and walk off down the street. But he seemed to see nothing where he was looking so he got in. Because Sergeant Brace had taken the shady side, Adelaide and Annie Mae had to move while Private Reagan squeezed in behind. As he did he reached with one hand and tweaked Annie Mae's nose, leaving his thumb between his fingers as if her nose were there. The one time Roy had done that Annie Mae had cried for two days. It was nearly a week before they convinced her that her nose was still on her face because she didn't really understand the mirror very well. Therefore when Annie Mae smiled, made the gurgle noise that he knew was laughing, Roy had to turn away and blink his eyes. He wasn't even able to glance at Adelaide. It suddenly seemed very clear to him that Private Reagan signified something and that this was going to be a significant day. He nodded, unhearing, as Sergeant Brace said that regrettably he had official business in the city, and would have to leave immediately following the service.

As they entered Barstow, Sergeant Brace asked Roy if he wouldn't like to have a nice cooling drink. Roy thought not, but said he would be glad to park the car a moment while Sergeant Brace stepped in and refreshed himself. So Sergeant Brace refreshed himself with three Cuba Libres. After that he felt better and was very cheery over the mountains and talked in a soft voice about places he had been. There were not very many but he remembered their names very well. There was the Hotel La Fonda in Santa Fe where he had been in the lobby with Errol Flynn, and the Hotel Pennsylvania in New York. Nothing had happened there but the feeling persisted that something would. He told this story so well that people begged him to finish it, although he had finished and there was nothing more to tell. They always felt that he was holding out on them. Recently he had found that that was a good way to leave it—and from there to tell them something else. It still struck Sergeant Brace rather queer that the only time men were terribly lonely was when they were cooped up like sardines in a camp. When a little drunk he always mentioned this—largely because he never stopped thinking about it and not because it always made an effect. It never failed to have an effect and create the impression that Sergeant Brace, underneath it all, was a lonely man. A lonely and a thoughtful man. A girl in St. Louis was still writing him because of that. But as a matter of fact no woman interested him any more than this one in the front seat. And that was about all that a man could say. In five hours all he had seen was the back of this woman's head, her neck raw from a shaving, and her hair like the oiled head of a mop. And for the first time he really noticed a woman's hat. The unspeakable silliness of it with its soiled sprig of feathers and the wax cherries forever bouncing on their wire stems. And to think that a man, even this man, lived with it. For a moment he felt a little sick and put his head out the window just as they pulled up to a stop sign. A man stood there on the corner and when he saw Sergeant Brace he opened his mouth, raised his hand, and said, "Hi!" This was just what eight out of ten men anywhere would do. There were always exceptions like Private Reagan—but Sergeant Brace had more or less proved that eight out of ten men naturally took to him. When he got to the city that was what *nine* out of ten men would do. People automatically stopped beside him and asked him for a match or the directions, and if he liked them and wanted them to stay, they stayed. There was no explaining something like that. People without halitosis and B.O. were sometimes the loneliest people he had ever seen, while he had them both and these sweet-smelling people would follow him around. This way he had with people was a very interesting thing and sometimes he wondered why it was he didn't use it. Instead of standing on corners, maybe he should lead people somewhere. Whenever he saw ads in the paper—*Man Wanted Who Can Handle People*—he always felt he should answer them. But whenever he got to the office, or stood in line, he lost interest, or got to feeling as he did sitting here.

For the one thing he couldn't stand was to be among people but not *with* them—as he was at camp and in the back seat of this car. To be uncomfortable with them and nothing else. And with people like that he was going to a funeral. Somehow he had thought so much about the city that he had forgotten how he was to get there—or that a man actually lived with a woman like *that*. The very idea of a funeral was too much for him. Once more he put his head out the window just as they passed a sign reading:

BEL AIR

The Oxford of the West

There would be no drinks there, and he sat back while they passed through it, or by it, since it seemed to be south of the road. But less than a mile down the road there was a sign. He leaned forward toward Mr. Herkimer, but Mr. Herkimer seemed to understand, for he was slowing down and pulling off the road. As he stepped from the car Sergeant Brace asked if they wouldn't all have a drink on him, as he had never felt more certain, so absolutely certain, that nobody would. But Private Reagan awoke from what appeared to be a sound sleep and got out of the car. Before he turned away Sergeant Brace inquired if he couldn't bring the little girl something, but in a loud voice Mrs. Herkimer assured him that he could not.

So, with Private Reagan, Sergeant Brace entered the bar.

As they came in the door Sergeant Brace dropped five nickels in the juke box, picking out Boogie-Woogie and any thing he thought would be good and loud. Anything that would keep him from having to talk with this chaste-looking Reagan—a boy that he knew, personally knew, still wet his bed. One of these kids still scared to death to be away from home. To talk to a boy like that about plain and simple matters was to end up with a man on your hands who had wet his pants. Luckily, this bar wasn't empty, and Sergeant Brace picked a stool beside a Marine who looked fairly promising. To the barman Sergeant Brace said to give his friend, here, whatever he wanted, and he heard his friend order Seven-Up. Not on the side—just plain Seven-Up.

On the counter beside him Private Reagan found the front page of the local paper, and read that he was in the town of Bel Air. The front page of the *Bel Air Advance* was soiled with many beer moons, and in one of them, as through a port-hole, Private Reagan saw a group of men. Two rows of men standing before a filling station. Over the head of one man was an arrow, and beneath the photo was the caption—

MISSING MAN NAMES
LOCAL LADY
NEAREST KIN

Missing since early March, news has been received that Agee Ward, promising local artist, has named Miss Augusta Newcomb as nearest of kin. A native of

Nebraska, Mr. Ward came here several years ago, after many years of study and travel abroad. Many people will remember Mr. Ward as the author of the poems *Chain of Being*—and for his colorful murals in the left wing of the new Library.

A native of Chagrin Falls, Miss Newcomb came to Bel Air more than twenty years ago. She is at home at 711 Via Bonita.

Returning to the picture, Private Reagan studied the face beneath the arrow, a very dull-looking face with a moustache and unseeing eyes. A mistake, obviously, but a thing to marvel over, and Private Reagan held the paper nearer to the light. But he was distracted by the face of a boy in the front row. A boy—or rather a youth, since he was going off to war, and standing directly in front of this so-called Agee Ward. But the truth was that this youth *did* look like him. That was a mad thing to say—it had been twenty years since Private Reagan had seen him—but if Agee Ward was in this picture who else would it be? Who else? But right at that moment Private Reagan's hat fell over his eyes when somebody slapped him squarely on the back.

"Honest to Christ," said Sergeant Brace, "why the hell didn't you order something a man could drink?" Sergeant Brace waved his hand at the stale Seven-Up—a full glass of it, not a bubble rising. "If you'd ordered a man's drink, why then bygod I could still drink it, but I'd as soon gargle a nightpot as sample that!" So saying Sergeant Brace turned and cuffed his friend the Marine, and the Marine obligingly cuffed him back. To the Marine Sergeant Brace said, "Well pal, we got to get goin'—Flash Reagan an' me are goin' to a funeral!" and he reached and pushed Flash Reagan off his stool. All in all, Sergeant Brace felt keen as hell, and he ordered a bag of the green-colored popcorn for the "little girl he had waitin' in the car." That was the one o sneak out on and he pushed through the door to where the heat and light fell over him like a black hood. For a moment he thought he was suffocating, then he heard Mr. Herkimer call, *Here—here!* and he put out his arms and walked blindly toward the car. As he fell in he remembered the green-colored popcorn. Over the hat with the bruised cherries he tossed the popcorn to Annie Mae—and promptly, as if it had bounced, it was back again. As if he were eaves-dropping Sergeant Brace heard—*It's plain to see that you're not a father!* and he found himself wondering, as the car started, who that might be.

4

As she pinned up her dress Aunt Elsie couldn't help but remember what an awful time with Grandma they had had. Overnight she had grown so absent-minded that she thought she was back in Paoli, a place she hadn't been in since she was a little girl. She would ask in a loud voice who these old ladies were she was living with, and who in the world it was that brought them in. Or she would just go off for a walk and turn in and visit all sorts of people, just ring the door-bell and say she was coming in. Colvin was a very modern little town of nearly twenty thousand people, and it was just impossible to explain that to everyone. She could never remember where she lived—except that she knew it *wasn't* Colvin—

and she usually gave her Paoli address and her maiden name. But the time she was gone all night, then found in the bus station talking to soldiers—after that it was clear that *something* would have to be done. Uncle Ben thought that the trouble was that the house was too small. Grandma was so used to living alone with thirteen empty rooms around her that having to live with people just got on her nerves. So at all the trouble and added expense of doing something like that in wartime, they added a room with two sunny windows on the west. And on the first day of spring Grandma had moved in. And from then on there was nothing but the problem of trying to keep her there. The very first night they left her alone she walked right out into the dark and was eight blocks away, in her nightgown, when the police car picked her up. But if they dared to lock her in she would pound until they let her out. And if they didn't lock her in they never knew what the morning would bring. The Gospel truth was that they were just worn to a frazzle when she died. If she hadn't died right when she did it would have been Uncle Ben, or Aunt Agnes— or herself, as she sometimes thought when she couldn't sleep.

And yet she might be with them yet if she had listened to Dr. Griggs. It was just the funniest thing how much she disliked him; *that man* was all she'd ever call him even to his face. She wouldn't let him listen to her heart or get anywhere near her, and she wouldn't take the medicine he had pre- scribed. They had to tell her it came from a doctor at home. They had to wrap everything up and put it in the mailbox addressed to Mrs. Lucinda Herkimer. Otherwise she wouldn't swallow anything. Not *any*-thing.

Remembering the black coat would need to be aired, Aunt

Elsie walked into Grandma's room—walked right in, as she said later, and didn't mind at all. Perhaps she had dreaded that more than anything. Grandma herself would be taken away and you could visit her when you felt like it, but a room was part of the house and would have to stay. And here she was in it and she didn't mind at all. She even thought that she would make it her own room as well. This would have seemed impossible yesterday, all day right up until she died, and perhaps for a little while afterwards as well. Until she told Uncle Roy how Grandma had died in her sleep. It was then that she saw that Grandma hadn't died. Just passed, as she said, and there was simply no other word for it. In her sleep, and without them really knowing, she had passed away.

There was nothing morbid in the room at all. It had always been a little small, and perhaps that was what troubled Grandma, living as she had in a house with thirteen rooms. But there were two sunny windows and bright flower prints on the wall.

It was too bad Grandma had never seen where she was going to be. Sunny Slope, with its unobstructed view of Colvin and the valley and a tree planted where it would give summer shade. And the one plot would be big enough for them all. Whoever was next would lie to her left and the next one to her right, and depending on future arrangements the last one could lie either way. If it was Aunt Elsie—she would rather lie on the right. There was always something about the left that——

Aunt Agnes stood with the flowers she had just brought in from the garden and waited until Aunt Elsie brought her the bowl. How much quicker she came, now that Grandma was gone! If it hadn't been for Elsie she wouldn't have known what she would have done, but on the other hand Elsie did some things too well. There was no excuse for sitting by the hour reading to her. When she asked Grandma five minutes later what it was Elsie had read Grandma never remembered a single word. She even forgot that Elsie had read to her. When a person gets like that the thing to do is leave them alone, close the door and sit somewhere on the outside. But Elsie had always been Grandma's baby girl. Well, that was all right with her since she certainly didn't have time to take care of Ben and Grandma at the same time. Somebody had to take care of the living too. That might sound pretty hard to say even before they had buried her, but anyone who had lived with her knew it was the truth. Grandma had made up her mind to die. Aunt Agnes knew that from the day Grandma didn't recognize her, which is a familiar thing with people waiting to die. They don't even want to live in this world at all. The only decent thing to do is make them as comfortable as you can and then be so good as to leave them alone. Dr. Jones practically said as much. But there was no telling that to either Ben or Elsie, any more than there was to complain about the lot. Just over the hill the same ground was one-third the price and she really liked the view better from there. Not that it would do them any good—but if they insisted on talking about it, then it was plain the other view was better than this. And to lie in the sun! As a matter of fact she would like it shady, as anyone would who had watched the grass burn out there. It was the hottest place this side of—well, it was. And though people died all year round she had never heard Mr. Lakeside talk about Sunny Slope except in the spring. It was just like him to have a Shady Slope off somewhere. A cool, shady slope where he could tell people who died in the summer that it would always be cool and shady there. She had never liked people anyhow who take your hand in one hand and then put their other hand over it. Perhaps it was very tender and consoling but she didn't like it. The palms of Mr. Lakeside's hands were always moist and perspiring and, as she had remarked, it was the same with the top of his head. It made his wispy hair look greasy and no matter what she had on, she always felt she should have worn something else. Sometimes something more, sometimes something less. She would rather have had the service out of town, or any place but a block from the corner where Grandma had stood in her nightgown that night. But, so long as Ben and Elsie were satisfied—now at last they could settle down where they were before Grandma happened—happened in on them the way she did. The rest of them would be along soon enough. If she wasn't careful it would be Ben, working himself overtime in a grocery, when at his age he should be the one in Grandma's room.

Sometimes Uncle Ben thought so too. Picking up the lamb chops for supper, he looked across the store at Mr. Bickel and waited for Mr. Bickel to catch his eye. Mr. Bickel finally did and nodded to him. Not that he minded working like he did, for a man like Mr. Bickel—but now he couldn't seem to work like that though he wanted to. Even if he could last a year, the extra money wouldn't mean anything, and by that time somebody else would be dead. The better-class coffins might be higher even than they were now. The plot on Sunny Slope was paid for but now he wished that the tree had been bigger, trees that size too often died off out here. Without someone around to see they were watered, they always did. The idea of lying out there under the sun for eternity—or at least a long time—suddenly struck Uncle Ben as a very mad thing to do. He felt very hot under his clothes and looked about for a place to sit down. On the bench advertising Hoffman's beer he seated himself in a narrow shadow, sitting erect so that his face was out of the sun. It was a little early for flies but one of them kept circling him. His sharp knees stuck out into the sun and Uncle Ben remarked that the pin stripe was gone, the very stripe for which he had bought this suit. Very likely that meant that it was also gone from the seat. And underneath that was very likely how it was with him.

He thought about that a while and saw how many ways in which it was true, and then, as he was about to get up, he thought of Grandma. Oddly, that didn't fit her at all. She was certainly worn threadbare, but none of the threads wore out; rather they wore in, the fuzz wore off and there they were. Of course one could say her mind wore out, but he had always had the feeling that it hadn't, that she merely put it away. Came a day and she just up and put it away. From then on he had known that there was no touching her, nor hurting her with anything they did. And from then on there had been no pleasing her either. She had just gone to bed and that was a kind of signal that she had finally dispensed with them. Uncle Ben had always liked her, but, if the truth were known, it would be that he had always been a little bit afraid of her too. For thirty years he had expected they might hear anything from her, and though it never came he always expected it.

Yet he could never say just what it might be. The more specific he tried to make it, the sooner it seemed to be wrong—it was just that there was always some unfinished business about her. At a certain age most people stop, they close the books and balance the ledger, but he knew that Grandma had never done that. Sometimes he wondered if that was what she feared. For she did fear something, something she found around their house, something Agnes called order and efficiency. Whatever it was he was sure it had scared her to death. As sure as God made little apples there was something in the house that scared her to death, but there had been nothing that he could do about it. Nothing. It scared her out of the front room into the bedroom on the side, then into the new room where she was cornered and scared to death.

As he got to his feet the noon whistle blew and his left foot seemed to splinter on the walk. He leaned on the light post and tapped his foot on the curb until it came awake. As he crossed the street he pushed up his glasses and slowly wiped down his face, drawing the palm of his hand across his mouth and chin.

5

At a stop light in Pomona, Private Reagan, who had been dozing, leaned forward and tickled the fuzz on Annie Mae's ear. He did this as a man who had pledged this deed in a dream and interrupted the dream to carry it out. When Annie Mae turned, he tweaked her nose off her face again. The expression that Roy then saw on her face was so extraordinary that he put out his hand and pulled to the side of the road. There Adelaide shook her because she was sure she was holding her breath. But Annie Mae was breathing all right and nothing seemed the matter with her. Nothing except Private Reagan. She wouldn't take her eyes off him and that wonderful smile strangers thought so angelic remained as it did in the photograph, frozen on her face. Looking at Adelaide, Roy thought he should say a word to Private Reagan before this had gone too far, but when he turned, Private Reagan seemed to be asleep. He was lying back with his cap like a hood on his face. Annie Mae was watching him in the rear view mirror, still smiling.

Adelaide admitted she didn't know what to do. This meant that she was free to ask Roy, that she could hand the child over to him, but one couldn't do it with a drunk stranger in the car. She folded her brown hands in her lap and edged herself a bit toward the door, making it clear that the problem was not just hers alone. In the windshield of the car she could see Annie Mae's face, the unblinking eyes as if they had been crying, but the wide full mouth in the gentle, frozen smile. For thirty miles, since Private Reagan had touched her, she had been that way. In that time Adelaide had combed her hair, scolded her soundly for picking a scab, and talked to her very loudly of everything she had seen. But for all she knew Annie Mae had neither seen nor heard anything. Here they were, just nine more miles to go, and if she was still smiling when they got there she would have to take her into the bathroom and do— something. Sometimes a bath or letting her wash her hands would do something. But she would undress her and put her to bed before any child of hers went to a funeral with that kind of a smile on her face. It was a nearly *indecent* smile if you asked her. In a book of pictures she had seen statues of nude women who smiled very much like that. Naturally, no one would accuse a child—but it was no smile to wear to the funeral of a grandmother who was very fond of her. They were so fond of each other she had asked Roy to take her away. There was something unhealthy about that too, the way that a nearly hundred-year-old woman and her little girl liked to sit or walk around. They had broken up a two month visit to one month because of that. Never in the world was there a situation like the one they had that summer, with two people you couldn't really talk to sensibly. It was just impossible to tell whether they were listening or not listening, or if they were listening but did something else anyhow. Morning to evening they were together all the time. When it got to where Annie Mae wouldn't sleep unless Grandma was in the room with her, even Roy could see that it was time to take her home. She expected her to cry all the way back, but instead she smiled all the way—she had forgotten that, yes, Annie Mae had smiled then too. That was the first time she had ever smiled because they were taking her home, but she had stopped smiling the moment they drove into the yard.

As they crossed the railroad tracks Adelaide put her hat back on. If Annie Mae was still smiling she would take her inside and straight to the bathroom, which would be natural, and they would stay there until the smile wore off. Having a plan made her feel better and she leaned forward until her nose and the fuzz on her lip were visible in the glass on the clock. Then from her bosom she slipped a small puff and a little wildly powdered her nose. Before putting the puff back she touched her cheeks, her eyebrows, and the lobes of her ears.

For that—for that if *for* anything, Roy had married her. For the little puff that disappeared in her dress and the mystery of the ear-lobe ritual. After fifteen years still a mystery. But at home, uncorseted, there was no place for the puff, and put aside with it also was miracle and authority.

So that she would not get carsick on the back road into Colvin, Roy had driven around the long way. From the cool north side they drove slowly into the sun. Shading his eyes Roy looked at the smooth slope of the hill, a sunny slope—green with spring rains, but a little vacant. Looking closer Roy could see that the shadows were cast by gravestones, and near the front were a few shadows without any stones. Graves, newly dug graves—hmm. The word *fresh* came to mind, but with it a vague distaste that he should have thought of a word like that at all. That was the fault of the red earth piled in a mound at the side, and the shot of dirt that periodically rose from the hole. He turned his head with the intention of calling Adelaide's attention to what he thought would be a pleasant place to lie. But a passing glance at her changed his mind. He hadn't thought of it at first, but there just might be something revolting about digging graves in public like that. For the sake of people who felt like that, people like Adelaide, they might put up a screen with something pleasant on it. They could paint it to look like a tree or a bright patch of flowers, and from the road you would never know the difference. And people who happened to be going to a funeral as they were, wouldn't be reminded of how much dirt there is in a grave. And how much of it they shovel back on you.

At the corner of Beverly and Orange he turned east and went into Colvin, avoiding by six blocks the home of Mr. and Mrs. Boles. He waited for Adelaide to comment but sometimes she showed an understanding that he never really expected of her. On the shade side of the Bus Depot he got out and walked around to the window where Sergeant Brace's face lay under his hat. On the back of an unpaid cleaning bill he wrote Mr. and Mrs. Boles' address and the words, "Leaving tomorrow—ten o'clock." Then through the window he said,

"Well, Sergeant, here's your stop."

Sergeant Brace awoke from his sleep to wonder where he was and how he got there, but the only place in his mind was the Oxford of the West.

"Bel Air?" he said.

"You bet," said Roy. "Do you good." So Sergeant Brace relaxed and they dragged him from the car. With his arm around Private Reagan he went through the sun into the Bus Station, and on the last stool at the lunch counter they settled him. They left a quarter on the counter for black coffee. It was the opinion of Mildred Bell that he wasn't so drunk as he was carsick, or carsick *and* drunk, which wasn't so bad as it looked. Anyhow she would look after him. Into his pocket on the left side, the tip showing, they left the address—with the understanding that Mildred would call his attention to it. Then they left, and Sergeant Brace tipped his hat over his face.

6

For people over ninety years of age Reverend Horde had a special service, considered his best by those under ninety as well. It had been inspired by the death of his mother who technically died at eighty-nine, but whose service was held over to her ninetieth birthday. This service expansively recon-

[38]

sidered the manifold blessings of a long life and the Peace to be found with a just and merciful God. Admittedly, it suited his delivery very well. This delivery was founded on the use of the voice as a religious instrument—a definition that Reverend Horde contributed himself. Standing in the living room with Mrs. Boles and gentle Miss Elsie Herkimer, he was employed in tuning this instrument. It sounded good—this he could see in the faces of the ladies but above all in the look of Private Reagan. In fact, Private Reagan slightly embarrassed him. The way the boy stared—he was either very piously brought up or had been deeply moved by the passing of Mrs. Herkimer. If right now—at this very moment—he could speak to that boy, alone! Something like that would be worth a year or two of the Epworth League. These young people merely smiled at him, or were little potted saplings of their elders— and Lord, were there ever so many elders in the world as now? Was there ever in the history of man so many old and ageing people who came to the church to lean on it, not to help it stand? Who, when he spoke, would put up their hands and suspend from his words like straphangers, and when he stopped talking would collapse in their seats again?

It would help, it would be a great help, to know this young man was there. Young women could be found—but young men leered at him with the amusement of animals who have not yet dreamed that they would die. Only once in ten, twenty years was there a face like this. It might be the war had brought it to him—but for every face like that there were ten thousand valiant young pagans to laugh at him. The war brought loneliness and fear, but these men who wore Bibles *over* their hearts wore nothing more than a rabbit's foot, a charm. And they would lose their vision as soon as they lost their fear.

It was too bad that Private Reagan had a rather strange physique. Hard to say what it was, except that such a man in the pulpit would have the better half of his figure out of sight. Reverend Horde could not agree with these men—*men,* that is, and not Saints—who assumed that piety could overcome a dwarfish physique. Considering what a man in the pulpit stood for, and the number of times he stood alone, it should not be encouraged that certain people stand there at all. The ways to God were difficult enough as it was. Any man was free to save his own soul, but a man in the profession of saving others ought to make it clear that he is of the flesh as well. How a man lusteth after the spirit when a piece of the flesh is denied him—even when the flesh is denied him on his own bones.

With this on his mind Reverend Horde crossed the room to Private Reagan, thinking there was something, *something* that he must say. But the boy's wet stare unsettled him. There he had openly crossed the room to say something, the ladies were waiting, but all Reverend Horde could ask of him was the time. And then, like a fool, from his own pocket he drew his watch. At that moment the screeching of brakes distracted them all. Through the curtained windows they could see the taxi drawn to the curb, and as the door opened a man in a uniform backed out. Turning around to exclaim what a fine thing it was to have *our boys* present, Reverend Horde remarked the unusual pallor of Mr. Herkimer's face. Even the expression seemed strained, but that was a little hard to tell with his jaw and his mouth twisted that way. Then the doorbell rang and Mr. Boles crossed the room, wiping the palm of his right hand on the side of his pants.

In the bathroom Adelaide took off Annie Mae's dress shoes and her half socks, then held on to her as she put both of her feet in the tub. Never in her life was she so relieved as when she saw that smile change, become a smile such as almost any little girl might have. Any little girl who was shy and had her feet in cold water, that is. Adelaide was so grateful and relieved that she didn't say anything and for a moment just sat quiet on the stool. She would like to get into the tub herself, at least her feet in, but it was after three and the doorbell had just rung. Very likely that was the car for them right now. She dried Annie Mae's feet and between her long toes, then put her half socks and shoes back on. While the right smile was still on her face they hurried out. They went out the back way and walked all the way around the house because the other bathroom door was on the living room. And she could still hear the noise the water made. She was thinking of this and what she should say as they came in—when before she could stop her Annie Mae rang the doorbell.

For Roy—still where he was when Sergeant Brace had entered—it was the final proof of what he always knew about Annie Mae. There was no other word for it; she was there when he needed her. In the confusion of two doorbells the case of Sergeant Brace could be aired, since it was clear, quite clear, that he was not drunk any more. Plainly, he had come to ashamed of himself. His uniform looked pressed, even neater than Private Reagan's, and except for the gum he was chewing he looked just fine. There he was talking with Reverend Horde, each of them with a hand on the other's shoulder. Roy could see that was too much for Adelaide, knowing what she knew, but the other ladies seemed to take it quite well. The idea of a young man in the armed forces, friendly like that with a man of the Lord, was the kind of thing more people would like to see. Even the need to explain the sergeant's late arrival, or explain anything, seemed to be unnecessary. Roy thought he saw Private Reagan eyeing him with something like admiration, but his blue eyes were so faded it might have been something else. Private Reagan himself seemed to be right at home. If in all the room Roy had been asked to name someone that had lost somebody—then found him—he would have to name Private Reagan. Not that he looked sad—but there was just that look about him that Roy himself would like to have had. It was—well, a religious look. He wouldn't mention that to a soul; in fact, it lost something now that he had said it—but he was a little proud to have Private Reagan here. When he needed to reassure himself of the dignity of this occasion—as he did just now—why, then Private Reagan did it for him. So when the doorbell rang again he was fully prepared to meet it, and over the head of Mr. Lakeside he looked at the street. Perhaps Roy had expected a hearse—something with windows hung with black curtains and an urn, or a bowl of some kind, sitting there. Perhaps he expected the carriage they had taken father in. Whatever it was, Roger Burns Lakeside had to gently nudge him aside and enter the room holding his hat and his cream-colored gloves.

"If the ladies are ready—" he said, and of course the ladies were.

[42]

7

To his wife, Roger Burns Lakeside once said that he had changed mourn to morning, and when she let it pass he said it to others as well. In due time it was said with rose-colored lights. The ROSE LAWN MEMORIAL GARDENS had a fine Colonial doorway with a polished brass bell and an escort of cypress in Italian urns. As a general rule visitors entered here and guests employed the doors at the side. As the ladies stepped from the limousine they passed through a zone of heat and glare to where Mr. Lakeside stood at an open door. Whether by accident or design the short walk from the car to the door—the gantlet of sparkling whitewashed light—became an experience the moment the door was reached. The change from the glare to the subdued rose was audible. The ladies murmured with relief and the gentlemen took breaths of the fresh damp air that the cooling system fanned on the backs of their necks.

Sergeant Brace felt sure they had sneaked in the side of some theatre lounge. In the thick rose-colored carpet even their talk dropped quiet, and after a moment only Reverend Horde's baritone remained. The room was small—quite small, in fact—but only as he sat down was Sergeant Brace aware that it was also *intimate*. Mr. Lakeside had seated the ladies on a large comfortable sofa fittingly upholstered in a matching shade of rose. On the inquiry of Miss Elsie, Mr. Lakeside described *this* as a rose madder, while the rug was more like morning rose. The walls more nearly matched the rug, but the glow that Sergeant Brace remarked on the ceiling was sunset rose—as was Reverend Horde's face. So, too, was Private Reagan, shading to morning rose on his nose, and even the face of Mr. Boles looked cheery and healthy again. Judging that he, too, must be looking rose, Sergeant Brace felt a little tired. As a gentleman he sat in the second row, right behind the shaven neck and the bobbing cherries, but rather than look at that he raised his eyes to what appeared to be a screen. This screen was transparent, like a shower curtain, and drawn before a small stage on which several objects could be dimly seen. The level of the stage and the subdued lighting were something Sergeant Brace had seen before, and as he closed his eyes it all came back to him. There it all was, the transparent curtain, and over it the sign:

WANDA
The Girl with the 21 Jewel Movement

So he opened his eyes just as the curtain parted on the stage. Standing among the flowers was Mr. Lakeside, with one friendly hand on the casket and in the other a piece of paper from which he was about to read. As they hushed he read who it was that all these lovely flowers were from. Sergeant Brace twinged slightly because he hadn't thought of that and looked somewhere else for distraction. Near him, against the wall, was a small table supporting a thermos and two clear glasses. Sergeant Brace was on the point of refreshing himself when he noticed two vials on the shelf beneath, one in blue glass and one in amber, and each in a silver holder. On each holder a few words were engraved. Leaning forward Sergeant Brace read the word PACIFIER on the amber—and the word REFRESHER on the blue.

Perhaps his recovery had been a little too abrupt? That, along with confusing associations and not too sympathetic a state of mind. Whatever it was, Sergeant Brace seemed unable to comprehend either the meaning or the humor of what he saw on the vials. He did nothing but lean forward and stare at them. It was there that Roger Lakeside found him as he left the stage to speak with the ladies, but first he stopped to pour Sergeant Brace a cool drink. The water was chilled and sounded refreshing in the glass. He handed it to Sergeant Brace, who seemed to be in need of something—but when he passed him again the Sergeant was still sitting there. He held the glass before him and seemed to be gazing in it—but he made no sound when Mr. Lakeside took it from his hand. As it was still cold, Roger Burns Lakeside carried it into the adjoining room, and as the door closed behind him, drank it himself.

8

In all her born days Aunt Elsie never dreamed that dying could be so pleasant, starting with sleeping and ending with flowers in a place like this. She remembered—no she wouldn't remember and spoil something as perfect as this with how they buried Grandpa in the mud. In all her life she couldn't see why dying had to be so unpleasant, and now she could look forward to it in peace. What a shame, what a *shame,* Grandma had not known about this. If she had had any idea she might have gone to sleep sooner—a week sooner than she did. To think—what hadn't they thought of here? Here they all were, sitting quietly together just as though they were at home and listening to the Ford Sunday Evening Hour. There were so many people she would have to tell about this. There was Winward getting on, and since one had to face such things how much nicer to face something like this. It did cost something, it *really* did, but when she let herself think of Grandpa —the rain patting on the coffin and the slosh it made when they dropped it in—well, when she thought of that she would pay anything, just *any*thing. Four into thirty-five—eight carry three—and into thirty-eight, nine carry two—wasn't bad at all considering what it was they——

Aunt Elsie turned—wondering what the trouble was.

Also wondering and turning, were Adelaide, Annie Mae, and Aunt Agnes, and at the end of the row Mr. Lakeside rose from his chair. As he was sure as sin it was what he thought it was, Roy did not turn. Nor did Uncle Ben who had known all this time.

Private Reagan seemed to be having trouble with his folding chair.

He was standing examining it, tapping the front legs on the floor, pushing on the back, feeling the seat, and doing everything there was no real need to do. There were more of the same chairs right against the wall.

Midway in the service for which he was famous Reverend Horde made an effort to continue, he cleared his throat and placed his fingers on his lidded eyes. He had been in the midst of that passage concerning the gentleness of death and he had been—he knew he had been—more eloquent than usual. The face of Miss Elsie Herkimer had been transformed with gentleness. And at that moment Private Reagan, the boy he had really had in mind—at that moment he should rise and start tampering with his chair. Reverend Horde waited, but as it continued he asked—without opening his eyes—if one of the gentlemen could possibly find Mr. Reagan a chair. Sergeant Brace did not seem to hear—seemed to have fallen asleep, in fact, but Mr. Herkimer and Mr. Boles were immediately on their feet. But Mr. Lakeside was already bringing a chair. Together they brought it, only to find Private Reagan sitting down, his arms folded, just sitting there. Incredible—but there he was sitting down. With wide foolish eyes he was staring at Annie Mae who could be heard, now, in the quiet, gurgling for him.

Had he conceivably behaved in such a manner to amuse that child?

Reverend Horde did not know, all that he knew was that he had no voice and an unaccountable languor urged him to sit down. Turning to the rose-strewn screen behind which Miss Ogilby awaited his signal, he nodded to her, and the room filled with *Lead, Kindly Light*. As he turned to leave the platform, get to a chair, find a chair, he was blocked by Mr. Lakeside on his way up. Holding his hand, Mr. Lakeside thanked him for the most happy address on the saddest subject that he had ever heard. Still happy, Mr. Lakeside propped up the Dutch-door lid that only the better caskets had.

The incident of Private Reagan had unstrung Uncle Roy. Uncle Ben knew this, but his own lip was so trembly he didn't dare walk over and speak to him. A few words about Needles and how things were going would settle him, but it wouldn't help if his own eyes were ready to run. Still, he ought to do something, and he turned with this in mind when Adelaide hurried toward him with Annie Mae. Into his lap she put Annie Mae's hand and there was nothing he could do but sit and hold it until she came back for it again. As it lay there Uncle Ben looked at it. All the times he had held this hand he had never had to watch it, or keep it from crawling around looking for things. It wasn't what he'd call a pretty hand—a little too long and bony—but there was something about it that he felt should do something. As much as two years ago he had said that Annie Mae ought to learn the piano, although he knew well enough that she couldn't learn anything. But you couldn't tell him there wasn't something that hand was for. Or Annie Mae, for that matter, with something about her that embarrassed him, for old as he was she sometimes made him feel brand new. As though nobody but Annie Mae had ever set eyes on him before.

When Elsie stood up, Uncle Ben turned to speak to Uncle Roy, to ask him to come and join them there on the soft seats. But Uncle Roy was no longer there. Standing there in his place was Private Reagan, who seemed to be waiting for a sign, and Uncle Ben was so surprised that he might have given it. Whether he gave it or not, Private Reagan sat down beside Annie Mae. At the same time Annie Mae removed the hand that Uncle Ben had been holding, for, when he looked for it, there it was, there both of them were on Private Reagan's sleeve. They did not grip his arm—just lay there, the fingers spread. Over her head Private Reagan was saying that he would watch Annie Mae while Mr. Boles had a farewell look at Grandma Herkimer. Uncle Ben did not care to look at her—but he thought again of Uncle Roy and got up to do something about it. But as he stood up he saw Adelaide, Adelaide with one hand on the casket and her eyes and her mouth open as if transfixed. She was not staring at him but at Annie Mae and Private Reagan, who were sitting, just sitting, where Uncle Ben had left them. Believing she was overcome with emotion—as well as holding up the line—Mr. Lakeside picked up the vial labeled REFRESHER and brought along a chair.

Aunt Elsie was both surprised and a little ashamed. A big strong woman like Adelaide, at least twenty years her junior, and not really related to Grandma at all. As they led Adelaide away Aunt Elsie had to pause until her eyes stopped blinking, a habit she had whenever she meant to say anything. Then she leaned over the casket and looked at the lovely white satin lining—looked at it first just as she did with the lining of Christmas boxes before she looked at what they contained. It was just a plain, simple way to get the most out of things. And a last look at Grandma was something that she had to get while she was here and make do until they were—heavens, she had forgotten all about that brooch. She would have thought Aunt Agnes would have told her, or hinted, or something without letting her come right on it at a time like this. Grandma had certainly picked it up in a dime store somewhere. She just hoped it was paid for—but anyhow there it was, big as life, and most of the gold finish worn off it too. It was more than likely Uncle Roy that wanted it there. Men were funny that way, and she was relieved to think that no man would have the final say-so about her. She would have it all white—even

[49]

though she didn't have the complexion for it—for white was certainly the gentleness of death.

On the chair Mr. Lakeside had brought him Reverend Horde was considering, for the third time, what he might have said to have made Private Reagan behave that way. But as Miss Elsie Herkimer left the casket and came toward him, he behaved in an even stranger way himself. He rose suddenly, as though someone had hailed him, and crossed the room to where Mr. Lakeside was backing in with a tray. On the tray were eight glasses of water, and as Mr. Lakeside turned, Réverend Horde helped himself and then went out through that door.

Uncle Ben was afraid that Aunt Elsie was looking for him. This thought gave him such a panic that he opened the door marked LADIES, before he noticed the one next door marked GENTLEMEN. He left the ladies' door swinging and went through the gentlemen's door so fast that he nearly knocked Uncle Roy off the radiator. There he was, standing, of all places, on the radiator, blowing the smoke of his cigarette through the window transom. But he went on blowing so there was nothing for Uncle Ben to do but go right on by him through a door somewhere. Only when he closed the door to his booth did he understand. A very large NO SMOKING sign was riveted to the back of the door, with the additional warning that THIS means YOU. But before he thought of anything to say he heard Roy go out. Uncle Ben didn't smoke, drink, or chew, but sometimes he wished that he did, and he felt pretty sure that Roy had just had what he needed most. But he couldn't smoke so he just stood there. It was quiet and cool, so he let the lid down and sat on it.

As Roy came into the room he saw Sergeant Brace and Private Reagan and, seated between them on the sofa, Annie Mae. On the chair by the thermos jug, where he had hoped to have seated himself, was Adelaide, holding a bottle of some kind. Her hat was pushed back and her eyes swung back and forth with the cherries that were now squashed down over the brim. That had happened before; it happened whenever she was distressed and her right hand would automatically pat her head. Usually that was at home and only her permanent was damaged, but away from home she always ruined her hat. And the cherries would squash down and swing under the brim.

But Roy did not feel like rearranging them—now. When he saw Mr. Lakeside, his head high as if looking for someone, Roy smiled as though it might be for him. Mr. Lakeside would have preferred Mr. Boles, but as it was already four o'clock and he had another service at four fifteen, he would have to let Mr. Herkimer do. It was simply a matter of what to do on Sunny Slope. As he was listening Roy saw an attendant mount to the stage and, right before his eyes, lower the coffin lid.

From the look on Mr. Herkimer's face Mr. Lakeside surmised what had happened and changed to a matter-of-fact discussion of embalming fluids. Most people had no idea—and it was the very idea that surprised them and gave them something else to think about. But what troubled Roy was that he hadn't seen her at all. He had come all of this way not to bury her but to see her, and now the lid was down, the man was sealing it up. But Roy recovered himself in time to hear what a fine thing it was that among the pallbearers were men in uniform. Regrettably, Mr. Lakeside said, he would be unable to be there, but his able attendant would see to everything. If he, Mr. Herkimer, would just see that four able-bodied men were handy—such as himself, Mr. Boles, Sergeant Brace and Private Reagan. At this point Roy turned and saw Uncle Ben backing out of the men's room, his hair wetted down and arranged in stripes across his pate.

9

The ride out Aunt Elsie remembered as very beautiful. The window of the limousine was so clear that her eyes sparkled in it, and they drove so slow that she could name the flowers as they passed—wisteria, iris, verbena, bougainvillea, and one Japanese cherry in bloom. Rather than break up their *little family*, as Aunt Elsie herself had put it, Sergeant Brace, Annie Mae, and Private Reagan sat in the rear. Annie Mae had given them each a hand, and although Sergeant Brace looked a little worn, it was plain that he had a fresh hold on himself. Private Reagan looked better than he ever had. There was something not quite natural about his face, Aunt Elsie couldn't help thinking, but it might be just windburn after such a long ride. Beside Sergeant Brace sat Adelaide, who didn't look well at all, then on the spare seats sat Uncle Ben and Uncle Roy. She and Aunt Agnes were in front with Mr. Grace. Aunt Elsie would have preferred that Mr. Lakeside had been driving, but she knew very well that other people died too. One could see that in the newspapers every day. Sometimes she really wondered—yes, she really did—where they ever made room to bury them all. Nicely, in a place like Sunny Slope, that is. Shading her eyes she looked ahead where she knew Sunny Slope would be waiting and where, if they could, all of those people would look down on her. At this time in the afternoon it was at its best. Not quite so bare looking, and the newly planted trees had shadows and didn't look so likely to burn as Uncle Ben was so afraid they would. Seeing it now Aunt Elsie knew that one of them should have told Grandma that this was where she was going to be. But whenever they went driving, or stopped for flowers around here, there was just something about Grandma that got in the way. You could *feel* it—it was right there and it got in your way.

As Mr. Grace turned into the drive Aunt Elsie leaned forward to see the new smiling Christ smiling at her. Then they drove in and out, until things looked familiar, but there was a mound that she didn't remember, all planted with grass. As the car stopped she could peek under the grass, as if it were a carpet, and on peeking again she saw that was what it was. A carpet of grass to cover the mound of dirt. That was just too much, for thoughtfulness that was just *too* much, and when they got out she rocked a bit and could hardly stand. But Mr. Grace was standing right behind her with a chair, just as if he had known that she was going to need one.

While Mr. Grace unfolded the chairs Reverend Horde stood with the ladies, doing what he could to comfort them. This was usually the most trying moment of all. The place was really so deserted—for himself he would rather lie head-to-heel in some crowded acre of ground than be lost out here. He would remember to specify that in his will. Not that these "Gardens" hadn't their points—even the hole itself was covered with a very lifelike strip of grassy gauze. All but a small hole at one corner where the gauze had pulled loose from the pin. So that this would not bother anyone Mr. Grace faced the ladies to the view, their backs to the grave and the grass-green apparatus for lowering the coffin.

And it *was* a very pleasant prospect at this time of day. Sunny Slope being new, relatively new, the slope to the valley was an unbroken lawn, not hallowed as yet by bones or carpeted with fireproof grass. From a little farther up one might see the sea—nobody present actually had—but they knew that they might and this knowledge was comforting. As they gazed, Reverend Horde was moved to turn to Adelaide, whose distress, of all the ladies, seemed the most real. She sat with her hands in her lap, and though she faced the valley she did not see it; a distraction as pronounced as a film lay over her face. Reverend Horde spoke to her about the winter at Needles, how much he sometimes felt drawn to the desert, and how he hoped Mr. Herkimer's ice business was flourishing. At one moment Adelaide raised her hand to her hair, as women sometimes do—Reverend Horde had observed—when they had something very unpleasant to say. But her lifted hand encountered the cherries, very much as if she had reached to pick them, and to spare her feelings Reverend Horde turned away.

The four able-bodied men were removing the casket from the hearse. The sun was bright on the nickel-plated hardware and brought up the pattern in the lavender plush, reminding

Reverend Horde, a little unpleasantly, of a tablecloth. This part of the service was fortunately brief; a few words, a prayer, and then they could depart. And as was Mr. Lakeside's custom, the casket would be lowered after they had gone. There was something in all of this that Reverend Horde did not like— and he liked it even less this afternoon—but what was to be done with people who were upset even by this? As a young man he had helped, personally, lower every man into his grave, and sometimes lent a hand with the shovel if it looked as if it might storm.

Remembering this, he walked to where he would stand and where they would deposit the casket, his own eyes facing the grave but the pallbearers facing him and the view. He took his stand there and, as was his custom, opened his Bible to help focus his mind, resting his eyes on the pages and letting the wind stir the leaves. As they made their way toward him with the casket he remarked that the two soldier boys were in front, Private Reagan erect and staring—and this some-what distracted him. A sudden fear that he might say—might find himself saying—what this boy didn't like, led him to close his Bible and slowly raise his head. What if this upstart had another impulse to rattle his chair? But as he opened his eyes he could see over the head of Private Reagan, over all of them, and he stared at the sapling just beyond the grave. For a moment he searched for some parable of leaf shoots, saplings, and the mystery of spring, but even while thinking his mouth opened and he began to speak.

"All life is Holy—" he heard himself say, "but its desire is to be immortal, and in mortal man this is the divine thing— that he might conceive. In mortal life it is conception that links man through woman to God, and she through God to him, and this is the Trinity."

Hearing this speech, Reverend Horde knew this was some kind of textual blasphemy—but he went on with his talking, or rather his listening, and this was what he heard:

"This is the Resurrection," he said, "that man should die so that he might live, that he should go so that thereby he might come again. For except a man be born again he cannot see the Kingdom of God."

At this moment, in a loud croaking voice, Private Reagan said—"*He has come again!*"

There being nothing else to do, Reverend Horde raised his hand in an attitude of blessing, thinking this might calm him, bring some kind of focus to his staring eyes.

"*He has come again,*" Private Reagan said, not very loud but insistent, and his croaking voice turned the ladies on their chairs. As they faced him, he faced to them and said, "*He has come again.*"

When Adelaide turned to look at the men and see who it was that was doing all the talking, she saw Private Reagan and beside him Sergeant Brace. Annie Mae was nowhere to be seen. She had left Annie Mae in their care because she was just too tired to argue and she had certainly, anyway, done the best she could. But Annie Mae was neither in nor under the car. She stooped to look beneath the hearse and when Annie Mae was also not there, she stood, very suddenly, and called, "Oh-h—An-nie Mae!"

As in a dramatic dialogue, Private Reagan turned to her and in a still louder voice cried, "*She has come again!*" This was too much for Adelaide, it had been a long day anyhow

—but whether she sat down or fainted, nobody—nobody was quite sure. For at that moment their eyes were all on Private Reagan. He had turned away from the casket and was walking, very erect, across the greensward between him and the grave. The flap at one corner was still open—a little more open—or so it seemed to Reverend Horde as he watched Private Reagan peer into it. As he rose, Private Reagan raised his hand, then, as a man who brings great tidings, he leaned slightly backward and away from the multitude. In a voice still croaking, but firm, he said—*"She has come again!"*

In a long life Reverend Horde had neither seen nor been visited by the supernatural, but he had lived knowing that some day he would be—and here it was. What amazed him was first his anticipation, and now his calm. It was clear that in the light of his vision Private Reagan tended to mix his pronouns, but this was the kind of thing that anybody might understand. All he feared was that one of the ladies might faint and have to be caught and carried somewhere, breaking a spell that all men awaited but few ever beheld.

Although Private Reagan had made no sign that anyone should approach him, Sergeant Brace was running toward him across the lawn. This was that understanding that surpasseth understanding—but Reverend Horde knew that he was not needed there himself. Just as if he knew what it was they would find there—up from the grave into the arms of Private Reagan came Annie Mae, her body in a curve with her head between her knees. With Annie Mae in his arms, Private Reagan immediately walked away. He crossed Sunny Slope before the transfixed ladies, all but Adelaide, who, happily, had fainted dead away. As it happened, the mound of earth, so thoughtfully covered with a carpet of grass, had been right behind her and she seemed to be reclining there. Not very attractively, for her hat had pushed over her face and the constant cherries were still bobbing up and down. All of this, however, Private Reagan failed to see. It was later remarked that he made his way to the limousine without actually looking; his eyes were open but he was not using them. He seated himself, Annie Mae in his arms, in the rear seat.

At that moment there was a pause that Reverend Horde feared might have been disastrous and broken with speech, but Sergeant Brace appeared in time. He had been left to shift for himself at the bottom of the grave while Mr. Boles and Mr. Herkimer stood as if dazed. But once out he walked straight to the car in just such a manner that it was clear to them all that it was time to go. In a very matter-of-fact way he climbed in beside Private Reagan, and it was observed that Annie Mae soon reached him a hand. That she was alive, had moved, made the rest possible. The ladies hurried to their seats in the car—except Adelaide, who was transported to a place with Reverend Horde in the rear of the hearse. The gentlemen took their previous seats, but so that Annie Mae would feel free to unfold, Sergeant Brace and Private Reagan sat alone with her. An attendant was left to supervise the burial of Grandma. This now seemed an afterthought, an anti-climax to say the least, now that Grandma had already come again.

Aunt Elsie couldn't help thinking that without the foresight of Mr. Lakeside something like this, a wonder like this, might not have occurred.

Aunt Agnes could not think, simply could *not* think, that

[58]

was all. She would have a cup of coffee, black coffee, then she would think. Then she would think what she would think.

When Uncle Ben was a boy he had buried the white hairs from a mare's tail in a can of sand, and the can in the bottom of a rain barrel. When the rains came there should be garter snakes. Once, when the rains came, there were.

Uncle Roy was not thinking. He was listening to Annie Mae who for the last five minutes had been talking. That was five minutes longer than she had ever talked before. True, she didn't seem to be saying anything. But Private Reagan was listening and now he was answering her.

As for Private Reagan, he was thinking of Agee Ward. It all began with Agee Ward—and now that he was Agee Ward he couldn't help thinking, he couldn't help wondering, where it all began.

THE THREE AGEE WARDS

FOUND AMONG AGEE WARD'S effects—after he was reported missing—was an album with pictures of his family and of himself. The first picture is dated 1892. As it throws the only light we have on the problem of where it all began, we will begin with the family of Addie Ward. The picture is signed:

Mrs. Addie Ward's Family
Christmas Day—1892

In the opinion of Addie Ward, there was a Ward at the Battle of Hastings—a Fitzroy Ward, or perhaps it was a Ward Fitzroy. More recently, however, there were Wards on a farm near Zanesville, Ohio—and the album begins there on Christmas Day, 1892.

Of Addie Ward's fifteen children twelve have come home for Christmas dinner, one being dead, one in Alaska, and one unclaimed. They have had dinner, and now they stand in a

[63]

fresh snow before the house, a long single row nearly spanning the width of the yard. There is something unnecessary in the length of this line. It is not a small family—but there is room between each of the men for another man, and in one instance room for two. They do not stand together as a family, but rather each man for himself, as if for his portrait, a zone of space surrounding him. Perhaps to counteract this, the photographer placed the two ladies in the center, and asked them to face each other while holding hands. But rather than join, this has merely divided the line. The gentlemen have first excluded the ladies, then set about excluding themselves, ten single portraits and one double being the result. But because of the length of this line, and the increase in the field of vision, none of these faces appears very large. And the details no longer appear at all. Even the dark eyes have faded into the all-pervading yellow—the yellow snow, yellow house, and the flat yellow sky. Only the row of Sunday-black figures is distinct. And yet it is clear that even without faces these figures are good portraits—the absence of the face is not a great loss. Uncle Harry Ward, third from the right, discovered this for himself. When he was a very young man and most of these figures still had faces, the only one he was sure about was himself. Himself and the two girls, that is. But when his eyes weren't so good and all he could see was how they were standing—why, it seemed that he knew them right off. As soon as their faces were gone he knew them right away.

This was how Fayette Agee Ward learned about them. When he learned about his father, his father no longer had a face. His father had a·stance—and it was Uncle Harry's opinion that no man, himself included, stood as well as his

[64]

father did. But it was some time before Agee Ward was aware of this. On his father's right and his left were Uncles Kermit and Mitchell, each doing more than just standing there. The twin brothers Alfonso and Lorenzo were more or less just standing, but nobody stood so well-standing as Henry Cleveland Ward. It was only natural that he learned to stand even better in time. Just as it was natural for Kermit Ward to stand even worse.

Long before he had remarked how well his father stood, Agee Ward had settled on Kermit—settled on him because nobody knew where he was. This explained why there was so much space around him. Only the girls stood together—but in this picture it might be said that only Uncle Kermit really stood alone. He achieved this by stepping backward one short step. This did not throw him out of focus but it did throw him out of line, much more than Uncles Harry and Mitchell who had stepped forward a bit. And that nobody knew where Uncle Kermit was—only the places where he had been—was also just as it should be. For these places had space around them too. He had been to war—to sea—to Australia—and to Omaha—and the last place he had been to was Rangoon. Agee Ward had never seen either his father or his Uncle Kermit—but it was his Uncle Kermit that he looked forward to.

From 1892 the record jumps to 1907.

It is a warm spring day in Nebraska, but we do not see much of it here as we are in SCHWICTENBERG'S PHOTOGRAPHIC SALON. Nor do we see it in the subjects of this photograph. There is a touch of it in the young man—where his hat sat his face looks a little faded—but the ladies might be taken for St. Louis belles. There is no explanation for this—these corn-fed girls were as we see them or this is an example of Mr. Schwictenberg's unrivalled art. The only problem was where, among five ladies, to put the young man. But this *was* a problem as it still shows in his face. We find him third from the left, his head turned as if from a blow, and a suitably stunned look on his face. For this occasion he rented the coat and bought the wing collar—but his role here is to emphasize how striking his little sister is. He is a pillar on which she leans, affectionately, but hardly to his advantage— and her high-piled hair is responsible for the odd tilt of his head. Except for her they all look to where the photographer holds the birdie, and except for her they are all thrilled to see it there. But she seems to see it within the camera somewhere. Or rather behind—since she looks through it and out at you. She is small, just a little girl, and some of her fine hair might be borrowed, for she is young, quite young, to be looking out like that. The face is a girl's face, but the look through the lens is that of a woman who has already settled many things. And there is a suggestion that perhaps you, too, need settling. That is clear—but it is not quite clear if this pretty girl, this wise young woman, has already settled for Henry Ward. It is only clear that Henry Ward will not settle it. All that we know is that she married him in 1909, and that the issue of that union was Fayette Agee Ward. After one day of loving him, knowing him, naming him—she died.

In the album of 1912 there is a picture of him. He is in a white dress and aged two years, four months, and eleven days. He is seated on a wire-frame chair of the kind popular in drug stores, and in his lap is a cage from which the bird has escaped. His fingers still pluck the wires of the cage but he has turned to complain that it is empty—or to look where the birdie now sits on the camera. His ears are large, and the one on the left appears a little out of line—where it remained regardless of all other changes made. Agee Ward did not notice his ears in this picture because of the curls, the long brown curls that hung from each side of his head. His ears stuck out, but not enough to hide the curls. This picture was glued down in the Album in the fear that he might destroy it, as he plotted—until he discovered something else. When he learned to read he found this information printed at the bottom:

Fayette Agee Ward
Aged 2yr. 4m. 11d.

He left the curls, but with his first knife he removed *Fayette*.

From 1912 we jump to 1922.

It is spring in Omaha, Nebraska, and we stand in the cinder-covered yard, facing the members of Mrs. Partridge's fifth grade class. The class is gathered at the side of the building, at the edge of the red brick walk, and between two small trees that are safely wired to the ground. The pupils are visibly arranged according to size and sex, but certain invisible forces have also been at work. The boys pair, the girls group, and the five Negro boys stand in a choir—except for the happenstance that they cannot be seen. Their shirts and pants are as if in suspension against the dark wall. The eyes of Mike Smith are wide open and like bolt holes in a stove, but those of Edward Dorsey were lidded as the shutter snapped. So were the eyes of Mrs. Partridge, who had turned to speak to Stella Fry, as she always closed her eyes when she had to raise her voice. She had to raise her voice because Stella Fry was holding up the picture, calling to her, and waving her hand in front of a small boy's face. This was because the boy was chewing something. As this photograph includes two floors of the building and a view down the street, the face of a small boy appears unusually small. And the smallest boy in the class has his face blurred.

We know who this boy is because the boy seated beside him bought two of these pictures and wrote the name *Agee Ward* across the blurred boy's shirt. His own name he wrote on the back. Anyone could see who he was; there was no need to write it across his shirt, so it was on the back that he wrote— *This belongs to Christian Reagan.*

Of Agee Ward's life with Christian Reagan several interesting pictures were taken a month before the class photograph. As there were eight pictures on the roll, Mrs. Reagan took the first four of Christian—Christian sitting, standing, looking and waving good-bye. In the finder Christian's teeth looked so white—she hadn't noticed before what white teeth he had— that she took a close-up of just his new cap, his new tie, and his teeth.

That left three pictures for Christian and Agee Ward. When they stood side by side Mrs. Reagan was amazed to see that one of Agee Ward's arms looked shorter than the other one. It was either that or his new suit had not been altered right. Nor had she noticed before how his toes pointed out. It made his feet look bigger than Christian's, and as big feet mean a big man it made him look bigger than he was. Without meaning to Mrs. Reagan snapped this picture too soon. Something went off while she was just standing there.

The feeling that this picture lacked something led Mrs. Reagan to arrange the last two carefully. As Agee Ward had one arm longer than the other she had him sit on the steps—but his hands either went up his sleeves or lay as if dead in his lap. So she gave him Christian's geography book. He was to sit and read it while Christian stood looking on. Christian was to stand in profile so that his feet would look bigger but with his face toward her to show his fine teeth. Mrs. Reagan took two of these just to be sure.

This record of Agee Ward is not in the album due to the fact that the camera shutter had not been wound. Mr. Reagan had never explained this to her. Once, by accident, she did wind it, and this was the time that something went off—but a little too late, however, and pointed at the ground. At the top of this picture can be seen two pairs of feet. Out of the roll of eight pictures Mrs. Reagan received two pairs of feet—and the big feet belonged to the smaller boy. Because of this she put off further pictures until Mr. Reagan could take them, but before this happened a strange thing occurred. A man with grass stains on his pants knocked at the back door one April morning, called himself Uncle Kermit, and said he had come for Agee Ward. With his Uncle Kermit, Agee Ward rode away.

2

The night of April 13th a fat man and a little boy slept in their car on Menominee Street in Chicago. In the morning they walked through the park which they found at the end of the street, passed a statue of Lincoln, to where the boats had honked all night. From Michigan Avenue, Agee Ward saw his first Great Lake. Far out on it his first boat was there to prove that the world was round—and while he looked his first wave came in and wet his feet.

At the edge of this wave a new album begins. This is why we see him without his shoes and with his stockings tied around his waist, his feet a little stiff for it is early morning and the water is cold. He is wearing his cap—but racing style, with the bill behind him, where the sun is also and this is why we do not see his face. In his right hand, at arm's length, he holds a large dead fish. On the back of this picture is written:

> First lake, first boat, first wave, first fish.
> Uncle Kermit don't swim.

The next is dated May 19th, and a rubber stamp reads: THE DELLS—Wisconsin.

In this photograph Indian Scout Ward is at the stern of a birch bark canoe, prepared to paddle, and lying in the middle of the canoe is Uncle Kermit with a cigar. Uncle Kermit looks happy but not very comfortable. The large pop-eyes, which he got in the war, look very large and stare like a fish. The brim of his black fedora is wiped back and may explain why he looks so daring. A high wind seems to be blowing into his face. Indian Scout Ward looks neither to the right nor the left. He prepares to paddle and looks straight ahead where cardboard rapids splash and roll, and clouds of foaming confetti swirl and blur in the air.. On the opposite shore an Indian maiden calls to him. Nearby a fish leaps into the air and remains there, poised, while the powder flashes and Uncle Kermit feels about on his shirt front for his cigar.

From May until November the Album is blank. But in November there are three snapshots, and the first is Niagara Falls. Nothing shows in this print but the blurred figure of someone just passing and, nearly as blurred, a boy in knee pants at the rail of a bridge Both figures seem to be at sea in a storm. The boy's cap is pulled down hard and the bill is unsnapped and nearly covers his eyes. On the back is written:

> These wonderful falls are wearing
> away two feet a year!

The next snapshot is without comment. Agee Ward is seated on an elephant, a pith helmet on his head, and Uncle Kermit distracts the elephant with peanuts. Three small boys, sick with envy, look on from the side, and a clown without make-up on his face has stopped to smile. Behind the elephant a banner reads:

HAGENBECK'S WONDER SHOWS

and at the edge of the focus two midgets in trapeze suits are holding hands.

The third is taken on Thanksgiving Day where Washington crossed the Delaware, twenty yards to the left of where Washington actually crossed. Agee Ward is seated at the steering wheel of a car with wire wheels and a brand new California top. He wears a turtle-neck sweater with dark stripes on the sleeves, and a pair of racing goggles with rabbit's fur lining lie flat on his chest. He has removed one hand from the steering wheel to point at Uncle Kermit and what he has just written on the side of the car. This is: CALIFORNIA HERE WE COME! On the running board are three large cans, labeled GAS—WATER—OIL, and a large bag of sand is propped to hold the cans in place. A desert water bag hangs from a noose on the radiator cap and drips a dark stain on a new army-duck pup tent. In the back seat of the car, still wrapped in paper, is a new set of tires. Three slightly used tires are tied to the spare wheel on the rear, and a piece of inner tube dangles from one to the street. On the back of this picture Agee Ward has written:

> Washington crossed it in '76
> Uncle Kermit and me in '23

On the sixth of February, 1924, Agee Ward was 14 years old, 59 inches high, and weighed just 87 pounds. This information is recorded on the back of the snapshot taken that morning. In the picture Agee Ward stands pressed to a palm tree in the Los Angeles Pershing Square, his head erect, his back straight and his arms flat at his sides. So it was that he would stand when Mrs. Reagan measured him against the door. But on his 14th birthday Agee Ward is wearing long pants. They are new, and the price tag peeps from under his belt. As this is very serious business he neither smiles nor stares at the camera; his eyes are closed and he seems to be holding himself in. Perhaps he will look taller that way. Pressed to his sides, his arms curve in until he swells at the front like a sack, his pants bulging and his shirt ready to spill. Not only is he holding his breath, but it is clear that something is off balance, the palm tree, the Square, the Biltmore Hotel—or Agee Ward. And yet they are caught, all of them, before they crash. In the background a man feeding pigeons stands with his offering, his arm extended, and he, too, is caught—just in time, with the bird perched on his hand. Just in time, also, is a squirrel, and from a bench behind the tree a small boy makes a face and thumbs his nose.

A photograph of a house—that is all, just a house.

Or maybe it is an ark, for the land extends sea-flat and level, vacant as the sea, and falls away from the house as the sea from a swell. Within the field of vision there is not another object, not a pole, not a tree. Except for this house there is not another sign that anyone else ever liked it here, settled here, or left anything that would bring him back. Nor is there any sign of too much sun and not enough rain. Not yet. All there is here now is this house. It is a large house, a city house, and might have been mail-ordered and delivered—but the land is beginning to tire of it. The city porch is gone and only the scars where it leaned remain. Everything loose, not battened down, is gone—the shutters, the rear stoop, the loose clapboards near the ground, and over the window facing the camera five planks have been nailed. That is all that we have to suggest that someone might come back. So long as the planks remain, somebody might come back.

There is one more snapshot from this year. It is taken on Larrabee street in Chicago, in front of a Y.M.C.A., and seems to mark the end—or the beginning—of something. Uncle Kermit is once more behind the steering wheel. His face is tanned -and a little thinner, but his eyes look a bit more popped, or he may be holding his breath until the picture is snapped. He wears the same black fedora, but the brim has so often been wiped from his face, or blown back, that it will not come down. Agee Ward is not in the car at all. He stands to the side, his arms folded on what is very nearly a chest, and he is wearing white duck pants and tennis shoes. He looks a little taller, but this may be the pants, or the fact that the curbing is high and Uncle Kermit and the car a little low.

But the greatest change has taken place in the car. The California top lacks three panes of glass, the new tires are vulcanized, and a wheel with wooden spokes is on the right front. Of the cans labeled GAS, WATER and OIL, GAS and OIL have disappeared, and the word WATER is partly chipped away. Where the cans leaned on the car all of the paint has been removed and a large hole worn into the rear door. The windshield is shattered but held together with adhesive tape. Through a long crack in the top the sun comes down on the instrument panel and spotlights the rabbit's-foot charm on the ignition keys. It has been somewhere, this car—but there is more to it than that. It will not let you forget where it has been. For it is not a car any more; it is a character. Here on Larrabee street in Chicago it has hailed every boy that has passed, and no man has passed without a word or two with it. But some of the boys have stayed for their picture, now stand in line in the street. They do not resemble any of the boys we have seen so far. There is nothing quite like them in the portrait of the fifth grade. In this picture they are slightly out of focus, as this is a picture of the car and they stand behind it in the street. But we seem to see how they look even better that way. We do not see who they are—that is a different matter—what we see here is what they have been. In this picture they are like the names carved on the face of a public building before which tourists have stopped to be photographed. They stand like pillars with capitals that read HUNGER—FEAR—DESIRE—ENVY, and between them, like a street light, WONDER stands. And on the corner, also like a pillar, stands Agee Ward. Not Hunger—Fear—Desire or Envy—just Agee Ward. In this row of boys we see that he is the one without a name—which is to say that he is without a face. In this row of faces we see that he only looks like himself. And in this picture that is to say—like nothing.

This first picture of *himself* was snapped by a boy named Peter Spavic who had just stopped to see what it was that was going on. When Agee Ward asked him if he knew how to take a picture Peter Spavic smiled and said, "Sure."

3

Of Peter Spavic we have no photographs. But his name appears on everything else we find in the album—postcards, drawings, and enlarged group photographs. All of which Agee

Ward, for some reason, sent to him. Except for Peter Spavic the record might have stopped in Chicago—right where Agee Ward was preparing to begin. This preparation went on for three years. For the next picture we have is somewhere in the Panhandle, in Texas, and dated October, 1928.

A full-length view of a young man—partly in a brown suit. The cuff has been let out of the pants but there are still two inches of leg between the shredded edge of the cuff and his shoes. The sleeves of his coat seem to be half rolled on his arm. He knows this is very funny and smiles—and for this alone we would not recognize him, as there is room for little else in his face. In this picture it might be said to be his face. Not that it is such an unusual smile, but it is a truly remarkable mouth. It brings up the question of where in the world it has been until now. As a mouth it has not yet made up his mind—but it has gone far toward making up his face. He stands holding his bag, the thumb of his right hand hooked to his belt, and so casual a stance that his body looks out of line. This is something that he picked up from a threshing hand. It alone would make us wonder where we saw this person before, as the pants are on the stance, rather than on the legs.

But on the back we read that this is Agee Ward. It is October and he is on his way. *On my way*—it reads, but that is all. Behind him the house and the windmill blur, the empty land fades into the sky, and a spotted dog sniffs at a dark stain in the yard. *On my way,* it reads, and we can see that he leaves with a face—or rather a mouth that is making up his mind.

A photograph of the Eiffel Tower addressed to Peter Spavic, Esq. On the back of this card is the message:

> The only obscene women I know
> are in *Vogue* and *Harper's Bazaar*.
> Reflect on this.

Under these circumstances it is clear why Peter Spavic ignored the Eiffel Tower and hurried to examine *Vogue* and *Harper's Bazaar*. He reflected on this for several months—he reflected until he was nearly sick—but just in time he left Chicago for school in the West. He did not look at the Eiffel Tower post-card again. He took it along because Agee Ward had left him in charge of the Album—but he never noticed that it was a picture of Agee Ward.

In a photograph of the Eiffel Tower most young men are at a disadvantage, and this is also true of Agee Ward. He is wearing a smart gabardine suit with the popular action back and the new patent zipper on the fly. There is also a zipper on his shirt, and one on the inside of his coat, behind which are his traveller's checks and his passport. On page four of the passport is a photograph taken in Amarillo shortly after he gave up the life, if not the stance, of a threshing hand. In this picture his hair is clipped short and the seal of THE UNITED STATES OF AMERICA is stamped like a legend across his brow. It is in keeping with his crew-cut, his steadfast gaze. The face is young, boyish-looking, but in common with many pass-port photos there is a question as to whether he is a little cock-eyed. But whatever its limitations, this face has now got him out of one country and into those already listed on pages eight and nine. And now he stands with it before the Eiffel

Tower. In his left hand he holds a beret, either because he still finds it sissy or he has learned that his face looks better with some hair. He is leaving Paris because he is lonely, because of the way the French speak their language, and because of the literature at the American club. This literature was mostly *Vogue* and *Harper's Bazaar*. We know his opinion on this subject—if not how he arrived at it—and with Peter all we can do is reflect on it.

NOVEMBER—A card postmarked Salzburg, addressed to Herr Peter Spavic. On the front of this card is a stunning winter scene in the Bavarian Alps. On the back is a life-like drawing of a small-town privy. The door is ajar, and through the crack can be seen a small boy, meditating. His head is cupped in his hands and lying open in his lap is a large catalogue. A few torn pages can be seen on the floor.

DECEMBER—A foto-mailer postmarked Vienna, containing four enlarged photographs and a collection of thirteen cancelled Austrian stamps. A scrap of paper attached to the stamps reads—*for Peter*.

The first photograph is entitled BUDAPEST EXCURSION. There are twenty-seven people in this picture, but the first one we see is Agee Ward. This is because he wears no hat, his shirt is open at the throat, and around his neck, like a frame, he wears a life preserver. On one side of his head can be seen the word BUDA and on the other side the word PEST. A felt banner, bearing the legend OESTERREICH-ISCHE AUSLANDISCHE STUDENTEN KLUB, is held in such a manner that it seems to be a decoration on his chest. Lacking these tributes the other twenty-six people, both men and women, appear a little ordinary. But the word that occurred to Peter was *foreigners*. This was very strange, for the foreigner among them was Agee Ward. In the background were the towers of a foreign city, on the funnel of the boat was a foreign name, and twenty-six of these people wore hats, ties, and suitably foreign looks. These were the facts—but they didn't seem to mean anything. Whenever Peter looked at this picture he always had the feeling that Agee Ward was welcoming all these strangers to America.

In the next—SALON—OESTERREICHISCHE AUSLANDISCHE STUDENTEN KLUB—we see eleven people gathered about a small fireplace. Over the fireplace is a needle-point rendering of the Flags of All Nations. At the side of the fireplace is a reading rack with the daily papers of five nations, and assorted literature dealing with ten or twelve more. The Salon is rather small for the people of all nations, and the eleven in this picture somewhat crowd the fireplace. The four ladies are gracefully arranged over two chairs. The six young men do all that can be done with a very small fireplace; they stand, lean, and gaze thoughtfully at a small log. This is the picture—and ten foreign students are more than enough for it—but the eleventh stands behind the chair of a very attractive girl. His weight is over his heels, his hands are deep in his pockets, and he stands as if he were watching other men work. As in the case of the Eiffel Tower he seems to be here by accident—but since he is there, it is the others that look strange.

BAL INTERNATIONAL marks a slight change. The view is of the dance Salon with all of the costumed dancers gathered before the three-piece orchestra. It is the moment that Herr Pius Prutscher has loudly cried, "Unmask!" But before looking at each other the happy couples have looked toward the camera where the flash bulb has startled some of them. They have closed their eyes and appear to be squealing. It is a very festive soirée; the native costumes of all countries can be seen, including the two-pants gabardine suit often seen in the United States. This is worn by the only young man who does not face the camera. He is staring at the face of his partner—the girl behind whose chair he was standing—but no explanation is needed now that she is standing up. This is a figure made in the U.S.A. She is facing the camera merely because she had to do something, and she knew that her profile was doing her best.

THE WIENER WALD marks a change Peter Spavic thought for the worse. In this picture twenty or thirty people can be seen at a picnic in the woods. But though we recognize others, we do not see Agee Ward. This is the contrary of all those pictures where Peter could see nothing else, and he nearly stopped looking—then found him with his head in this girl's lap. We cannot see his face, but we can see that his legs are crossed and that he is wearing spurs and cowboy boots. This could hardly be anybody else but Agee Ward. In the foreground of the picture the bicycles are sprawled—all but one, this being a two-seater tandem which is propped against a tree. At the front of this tandem waves a small American flag. At the back is hung a large banner, so large that Peter was able to read—and to wonder about—the word VASSAR.

MARCH—A postcard from Gorizia, Italy. On the front of the card is the blue Mediterranean, and on the back is another privy. But this drawing is so sketchy, so unfinished, that without the first one Peter would not have recognized it. Three pieces of detail are photographically clear, but the privy itself has neither top nor bottom. Over a knothole in the door is a piece of tin, a tobacco tin, with the image of Prince Albert peeling but still recognizable. Inside, on the floor, is a catalogue with the top leaves curling in the sun, and on one of the leaves we can see a watch advertised.

APRIL—From the Hotel Reale, Capri, a very curious drawing on a piece of their stationery. This drawing contains a farmyard, a barn, a corncrib, a harrow, a row of huge trees, a hedge, and behind the hedge, at the end of a trail, a privy. The same privy, no more and no less, that Peter received from Gorizia.

In the yard are the remains of a croquet set—four of the wire wickets, a striped ball, a club, and one bird-spattered end post. On the barn the hayloft window is clear and in the window are several cats—but the roof of the barn and other details are left out. On the harrow the metal seat is drawn as if copied from a photograph, but the seat itself is in suspension and not joined to the frame. The crib is blocked in very roughly and under the lean-to roof is a treadle grindstone. The drip can suspends over the stone as the harrow seat over the harrow—and how the treadle mechanism operates is a little obscure. Beneath the stone, in a nest of dirty feathers, is a chill, white egg. The hedge is cut flat at the top and extends the length of the driveway, with a break where the trail to the privy goes through. This trail crosses the drive and enters a windbreak of great trees, the tops of which are not to be seen. There is a heavy undergrowth, and it happens that all we can see of the privy is the tin on the door and the curling leaves of the catalogue.

But what is the growth that conceals other things? The whole sketch is like a peeling fresco, or even more like a jig-saw puzzle from which the key pieces have been removed. One of the hardest pieces to fit has been the pump. It has twice been in—and once erased out—for either the barn is much too close or the pump is much too far away. This problem may have more to do with the weight of a full pail of water—*fetched* water—than it has with the actual location of the pump. The only solution to this was to draw both pumps in, reconsider the matter, and then take one pump out. This he did, but the pump that he left was where no sensible pump would be. And the one he took out was the pump in which he couldn't believe.

FEBRUARY, 1931—From Tarvisio, Italy, a letter addressed to Agee Ward in care of Peter Spavic, Bel Air College, Bel Air, Calif. The Royal Italian Government asked to be advised as to the whereabouts of an English three-speed *bicicleta*, which was to have left Italy by June, 1930. It had not left. The Royal Italian Government was therefore obliged to demand a payment of 230 lire, or evidence to the effect that the three-speed bicicleta had left.

MAY—To Peter Spavic, from Paris, an envelope with two clippings. The first is a photograph of what appears to be a sliced kidney, or a cross section of sweetbreads, but on examination certain objects can be identified. There are parts of a croquet game, a strip of hedge, a cream separator, a harrow seat, a white egg, a piece of soggy yard, and a pump. In the back, holding up the sky, is a row of topless trees. It is a painting, and the name of it is THE JOURNEY BACK.

The second clipping is entitled *Through the Hole in the Palette,* and is a column of short art reviews. The last review in the column is circled with a red line:

If you're a small-town boy—and who isn't—you better have lunch at Vathek's and see what he has on the walls. I think you'll find everything you've been trying so hard to forget. Most of us are over here because we're trying to forget something, but I think Mr. Ward is trying to remember everything. I think you'll find that he does pretty well. If I didn't understand it so well I might think it was Dada, but it isn't; he's just homesick as hell. But this boy's home is really far, far away. I get the feeling from this stuff that what he'd like to remember happened sometime before he was born. It makes me wonder what he thinks he'll find over here. If Mr. Ward was me, he wouldn't paint THE JOURNEY BACK, he'd take it —then he'd hurry back here and forget the whole damn thing.

NOW THE LAND WAS TALL AND green with corn or bronze where the wind sloped a field of grain, but the sky was what the land had memory of. When he was a boy there had been no sky, only cottonwoods. Now from the road he could see the hills, but when he was a boy there had been no hills. There had been cottonwoods, then more cottonwoods—then the sky. Now there were stumps in the high grass back from the road. And the sky came first, now that the trees were gone.

A car came down the road toward him so he pulled to the side, held out his hand. The man came up slow in an old Dodge touring, pulled on the brake. There was dust at the base of his teeth and a quid of snuff that his tongue passed around—he settled it in his lower lip and looked at Agee Ward.

"Ward?" he asked. "Harry Ward—you ever know a Ward that farmed around here?"

[84]

"Know?" said the man. "Did I ever *know*?"

"He's still around?"

"Well, what do you think?"

They sat quiet a moment, staring at each other, and the dust came up and went by.

"Well, I'm looking for him," said Agee Ward.

"You one of his people?"

"He's my uncle."

"Well—" The man leaned and spit in the dust. With his thumb he wiped the stain from the edge of his mouth, then rubbed it between his thumb and forefinger. "You born around here?"

"Just south—" he said. "I was born about thirty, forty miles south of here."

"I didn't think you was born around here." He leaned out to squint at him. "No sir!"

"His farm," said Agee Ward, "had trees—big trees."

"We all used to have trees."

Pointing, Agee Ward said, "Is it still down this road?"

"His farm's where it's always been," said the man. "You already come by it a mile or two." Then he leaned forward and released the brake, with his other hand lowered the spark. Both hands on the wheel, he looked straight ahead and let out the clutch.

When the dust had settled, Agee Ward turned the car and started back. In the hollows a stream of heat crossed the road, or far ahead lay in a pool dividing the land into islands of grass or rippling corn. The sunflower leaves were coated with dust, eroded with rain. On the right side of the road, rising from a thicket of spare shrub trees were three cottonwoods, their dead white limbs barkless and smooth. Above the squat trees the lightning rods still held up two sky-blue faded balls. As he turned in the drive three small pigs raced along the hedge. At the break in the hedge he parked the car and looked down the trail cluttered with leaves to where the privy, the door still open, stood. In the white slant of light on the floor was a catalogue, the covers gone, and in the draft the pages lifted, dropped again.

There had been a screen to the porch, now tracers hung dangling feathers—fresh Leghorn and seedy Plymouth Rock. Rising from a chair an old hen, her frayed bottom softly pouted, left an egg rocking—a chipped glass egg on a dirty sack. She crossed to where the screen combed her tail then hurried to wade in the dishwater scum. In the kitchen someone squeezed a rag and with a smooth, damp pass wiped a table clean. The rag squeezed again and a few drops fell into an empty pan.

He opened the door and crossed the porch to the kitchen screen. Aunt Sarah stood beside the range, her arms flat at her sides. In her right hand she still held the rag, but now she looked through the house toward the front, on through the window to where the heat blurred a field of grain. Her dress hung as if empty, curtain-flat on her spare straight frame. When he tapped on the screen she turned to see if *that* was what she had heard—then she turned away and took her teeth from a glass on the stove. Slipping them into her mouth, she turned and faced the light.

"Aunt Sarah?" he said.

She came to the screen and looked out at his face. Gathering her apron, she wiped her hands, then lifted one corner to cover one eye—with her left eye she looked at his mouth, then one eye at a time.

"I only got one eye now," she said. "Maybe if I had two I'd have remembered." She let the apron drop and unhooked the screen. "Now who are you?" she said, walking away, then at the stove she looked at him once more. He stood straight, facing her, in the hot, sharp smell of pickling beets. "Now who—?" she said.

He raised the flat lid on the range cob bin and looked inside. Strips of white kindling covered the cobs, the sniff of pine in the stale whiff of the cob house. When he turned there were wrinkles forming at the edge of her mouth. He remembered that Aunt Sarah never smiled—sometimes she laughed in a high cracked voice, but the smile she sucked in with her lip, held fast with her teeth. But these store teeth wouldn't hold; it slipped, and she turned to look for her rag. Leaning over the table, she wiped at a spot of light where the sun came through.

"You're Henry's boy," she said. "You're—Agee."

"Yes," he said, "I'm Agee."

"You was such a little tyke—" she said. "And how's your people?"

"People?" he said.

"Ain't you married?"

"No—" he said.

She squeezed the rag until a drop sounded, left it in the pan. Lifting a jar of beets from the stove, she turned the cap with a wire cap screwer—as the blood-red juice began to ooze she tipped it upside down. She placed it upside down on a *Capper's Weekly* and watched for a leak.

"You seen I lost my tree?"

"So many," he said.

"Oh, some was dead—" She crossed in front of him to the window and spread the curtains, looked out at the yard. A stump, knee-high, sat like a tub in the chicken-tracked dust. Out of the cracks fresh sprays of green rubbed their pale veined leaves on the screen. "Some was dead," she said, "and some was just cut to be cuttin'." She dropped the curtain and stood fanning herself. There had been trees—now a glare lifted from the road. Through it the ripe metallic grain seemed to rise from a field of water, the surface shimmering as through a window of wavy glass.

"How did you say your people were?"

"All right—" he said. "They're all right."

"But you're not married?"

"No—not yet."

"If you're not by now," she said, "what makes you think you're goin' to be?" He didn't answer, and she said, "There's no use your standin' here in the heat. I got to finish what I start but you might as well sit where it's cool. It's cool in front or in the yard."

She left him there to make up his mind and went back to the stove. He walked to the table and took the cloth from the water pail. There were two drowned flies and he skimmed them off, tossed them through the hole in the screen. A frowsy Plymouth rock with a cotton-fresh brood ate the flies and scratched at the wet spot. Then the brood disappeared, chirping, as she led them into the grass. Near the middle of the yard was a slanting end post for croquet, the colors faded, the round knob splattered with sparrow dung. He left the dipper floating on the water, covered the pail. Another white cloth covered the bowl of the separator, sour-sweet smelling and chalky with powdered milk.

"I'll just take a look around," he said, and pushed on the screen.

"You was such a little tyke," she said, "we never thought about your growin' up."

"Hmm—" he said, and walked out in the yard.

He tripped on a wire croquet wicket bent low in the weeds. A little farther he stepped on a ball, half sunk in the earth, the color bands chipped and faded. When he kicked it, it split like an apple, cave-smelly and raw. He carried one piece along for the smell and followed the hedge to the trail for the privy—the door was open but covered with a fine lacy web. The catalogue on the floor was open to a page of leather harness with shadowy horses all dressed up in it. He looked back toward the house, but the yard was quiet, no one was looking, so he got down on his knees and crawled beneath the web. He sat himself down on the small hole and looked out. He was taller now but the hedge had grown, obscuring the house. The sun-bright balls of the lightning rods stood alone on the sky. He picked up the catalogue and looked at watches for growing boys—but the one with the stem-wind compass was no longer there. Now it offered a long second hand and a very soft tick. There were shoes—but not with green uppers and brown leather patches on the ankle and toe. And there were ladies in corsets—but not so much like ladies any more.

He read about many things and looked at all of them. He brought himself up to date in the matter of watches, electric trains, bee-bee guns and flannel sleepers with the hands and feet sewed on. Then he left them there, and left the cobweb across the door. He followed the hedge back toward the barn, walking in the sun where the shade had been. The tall, hay-sweet grass was cluttered with rusty machines. The blades of the gangplow were pitted like bark, growing like roots from a tangle of weeds. He walked on the harrow and the frame was soft beneath seasons of grass. Through the large hole in the seat of the disc a sunflower grew, creaking like a hinge in the slow even draft down the drive. The gear shaft of a drag held up a finger-spread cotton glove, the squeeze release sticking out through the hole in the thumb. In the shelter on the crib three young pigs slept in the leaky shade. A setting hen stared at him a moment, then lidded her eyes. Blocking the entrance, but enough outside to burn in the sun and catch the rain, was a new metal wheel barrow with a flat rubber tire. Three pullet feathers floated in the bright puddle of rust.

As he walked through the crib the three pigs grunted—but none of them moved. A chill, white egg lay in a hollow of pin-feathered dung. On the shady side of the crib, in a weedy fringe of grain, he found the grindstone with the wide gang-plow seat. The leather treadle joints were soft with rain and there were two fresh pools in the seat. He sat down and, pushing on his knees, pedaled it. There was water in the hanging drip can and a soft moist center in the stone. As it screeched the pigs left, smashing the egg, but an old hen lifted, then settled again. She watched him sharpen his pocketknife and tear a hole in his pants at the knee. Then he sharpened the hoe he found hanging on the wall of the crib, and the hand-scythe he found buried in the grass. He polished the studs in the scythe's handle, disfigured three pennies, sharpened five nails. He put an edge on a harness buckle of heavy brass. When he stopped he could hear the hum of gnats in the shade—and there was a rich, smoky smell of flint in the air.

"A-geeee!" a voice called him. "A-GEEE!" At the sound of her voice the old hen rose and hurried off. She left a cobbled bed of brown eggs and crossed the yard toward the house, where Aunt Sarah stood at the screen. Agee Ward stopped at the pump for a drink. This pump was *before* the barn, and while he pumped he thought about this and tipped his head for the rising swallow sound. When it came he covered the nozzle with his hand and stooped to drink. As he stood straight and wiped his mouth he could taste the oil washed off the pump shaft, a drop of it spreading on his tongue. Through the loose well boards he could see streaks of light on the water, hear the long, far fall. Waiting at the screen, but not calling, Aunt Sarah patiently fanned at the flies. As he came up she let the screen close and covered her eye.

"You remember Adaline?" she said.

"Adaline?" he said, and stood as if thinking. As he spoke her name she stepped from the kitchen onto the porch. She stood straight, as if for her picture, a wide-brimmed straw pressed to her lap, her eyes wide and blinking expectantly. Her long black hair was drawn through a napkin ring at the back, fanning out again where her shoulders were firmly squared.

"I remember *you*—" she said, but without looking at him, her eyes away like a woman being fitted, the seamstress in the back.

"She's Will's wife," said Aunt Sarah.

"Of course," he said. "Oh, of course."

"We used to pick berries—" she said and, still without look-

[91]

ing, pointed to where they had. "We used to pick berries," she said, and wiggled her finger until he turned and looked. There had been an orchard, and beyond the trees there had been fencing rows of berries and vines. Now there was the sky, the vacant land and the sky. Around the stumps the land had been plowed and there was a fine crop of weeds. Taller than the weeds were the maverick sprays of corn.

"Of course," he said. "You were——"

"Having a baby."

"Yes," he said.

"Or did I have her? Yes, I had her. In June. Sixteen years ago in June, sixteen years and twenty-two—three days."

"I remember," he said.

Turning suddenly, she put on her hat and, leaning through the door she called, "Cally May!" She stood there, waiting, and a tall girl appeared. Licking her fingers, Adaline smoothed a bang on Cally May's forehead, then stepped out of the way. Cally May stood erect with her arms sucked in like chicken wings, her fingernails snapping.

"Who does he look like?" said Aunt Sarah.

"Like Grandpa," said Cally May.

"Grandpa?" he said.

"Your Uncle Harry," said Aunt Sarah. "By now your Uncle Harry is a grandpa too. But I'll swear I'm really blind, I'm blind as Roy's mare if that boy looks anything like Harry."

Cally May hadn't really looked at him before; now she glanced at him. She stopped snapping her fingers to cover her knees and pat the kilt-high hem of her dress. Turning in her toes, she closed the draft between her thighs.

"All this Grandpa means," Adaline said, "is how much she

likes you. Anyone she likes she thinks looks just like him. She thinks her nicest lady teachers look like her grandpa too."

Aunt Sarah reached into the kitchen and brought out the water pail. She passed it out through the screen to him and said, "I hope you ain't forgot how to pump a little water."

"Now how could a man forget *that*?" Adaline said.

"It's harder to pump a little water," Aunt Sarah said, "than it is to tell a live tree from a dead one."

As he walked away with the pail they remained on the porch watching him. In the quiet Cally May went on snapping her nails.

"Ain't you broke her of that?" Aunt Sarah said.

"Between snappin' an' chewin', I like snappin'," said Adaline.

While he stood at the pump a model T truck entered the drive and came back toward the barn. She was hot, and hissed a fine white spray in the air. At the end of the drive she cut left through the weeds and bounced and rattled over the harrow, clapped the boards in the drag, and waving the white glove on the gear shaft, rocked, spit, and died. Pushing up the spark, Uncle Harry Ward backed out of the cab.

Facing the barn, the sky, he said, "Ain't you a little thin for a Ward?"

"Some—" said Agee Ward, and lowered the pail. Uncle Harry's eyes were the sun-faded blue of his overalls at the knee and the paunch, and the whites were the time-tired white of the thread trim in the bib. He was thinner at the top but thicker, pear-shaped, at the bottom. There the weight had sagged and settled itself.

"But you're tall," he said. "If you wasn't so tall you'd not be so thin."

"You're looking fine," said Agee Ward.

"Dam near died," said Uncle Harry. "Ten, twelve years ago dam near died." He reached a tall spear of grass and was careful to draw it slowly. He put the fresh tip in his mouth and let the head wag. "Had to give up chewin'—don't know but what if I had it to do over I'd just as soon've died." He spit. "You married?"

"No—"

"You ain't married?"

"No—not yet."

"If you ain't by now it ain't likely you will be." He picked up Agee Ward's pail of water and walked ahead of him toward the house. His arms hung heavy, the palms back, and there was a cud-like friction between his thighs. Aunt Sarah was there waiting for them at the screen.

"Would you have known?" she said.

"Well—I did."

"But—" she said, "he ain't a Ward's look."

"He's the Ward line," said Uncle Harry. "You can tell a Ward just from his chest—it's the Ward line to have a full chest."

"But unless I'm blind," said Aunt Sarah, "that boy ain't the *look*."

Uncle Harry struck a match and let it burn down while he stood looking at him. "He's the Ward line, but now that I think, it's the Osborn look. He's the Ward line but with the Osborn look. It's Grace in him that's giving you that look."

"Grace—?" said Agee Ward.

"My, she was purty. Wasn't till her they put blinders on horses. Up and down in a buggy she was a thing to see."

"But them ears," said Aunt Sarah, "where'd he get them ears?" Adaline and Cally May came out in the kitchen to look at him. "Now where—?" said Aunt Sarah.

"Like Grandpa," said Cally May, and snapped her nails.

Taking off his hat, Uncle Harry rocked the dipper and had a cool drink.

Drawing a feather through the bowl of his pipe Uncle Harry leaned forward, tapped it on his palm.

"So you're not married?"

"No," he said.

"If you're not by now you likely won't be."

From the kitchen Aunt Sarah said, "I already told him that."

"Guess I did too," said Uncle Harry.

"Do you think," said Adaline, "Mr. Ward came clear out here just to have you people go on asking him that?"

"I didn't ask him what he came out here for," said Uncle Harry. "All I've asked him is what it's my business to know."

"As if who Mr. Ward marries is any of your business."

"Who he marries ain't—if he don't marry it is. Me an him," said Uncle Harry, "is the last of the line. If he don't see to it he's goin' to end the Ward line." Uncle Harry slapped his hand on his leg and looked at Adaline. She sat erect, tight, her empty shoes on the floor. Her feet were drawn up out of sight and her hands were on the bowl of her straw, quiet but firm, as if she held a live chicken in her lap. "I was first—and now I'm last," said Uncle Harry.

[95]

"You look fine," said Agee Ward.

"You look all right too," said Uncle Harry.

"To hear you men talk," said Adaline, "you would think Cally May wasn't the Ward line. You would think a woman couldn't be the Ward line."

"I was thinkin' of the name," said Uncle Harry. "An soon as she marries this Humphrey boy she's gonna be workin' for the Humphrey line."

Hearing this Adaline stood up, sat down, stood up. "Cally May, you tell your Grandpa right here and now that you got no special interest in that Humphrey boy. That you got no special interest in *any* farm boy!" Cally May snapped her nails and rolled her eyes. Then she stopped snapping her nails and nibbled on them. "I'd just as soon you snapped them!" Adaline said.

"If they was mine," said Uncle Harry, "I'd be eatin' them all day. I never seen a farm girl with such soft purty hands."

"She ain't a farm girl," said Adaline, "and she ain't gonna be!"

"I don't know," said Uncle Harry. "Strikes me that Humphrey boy would just about starve to death anywhere else."

Adaline put on her hat, slipped her bare feet into her shoes. She pulled the draw-string noose of the hat tight under her chin, but her jaw was working and it slipped, swung beneath. "Cally May," she said, "you go an tell your Grandma that your Mother is about to take you right home."

"Land sakes—" said Aunt Sarah, "and right when our people's here."

"What I want to know," said Uncle Harry, "is what is she gonna be?"

"A lady," said Adaline. She pulled her straw down hard, then wiped the brim from her face and looked at Agee Ward, then back at Uncle Harry. "Mr. Ward is a gentleman," she said, "and my daughter is goin' to be a lady!" Uncle Harry turned and looked through the door. "Cally May, I want you should ask Mother Sarah if she'd mind Mr. Ward havin' supper with us."

"My land no," said Aunt Sarah.

Looking out through the door Uncle Harry said, "I left a load of grain settin' an drove home. Sarah calls the granary an they tell me that there's someone important at the farm to see me. So I left my grain settin', came all the way home."

"Will ain't seen him at all," Adaline said. She stood at the screen, looking out across the yard. "Roy ain't seen him at all, and when he does see him he won't be asking what isn't any of his business."

"Cally May!" Aunt Sarah called from the kitchen.

"Cally May," said Adaline, "you tell Mr. Ward that your Daddy's on the combine until after six o'clock, but any time he likes he can come by and make himself at home."

"Yes," said Cally May.

"And if Mr. Ward wants to know the way, mind you don't show him by the outbilly!"

"No," said Cally May.

Pushing through the screen, Adaline walked across the yard. She walked with her head down, her arms crooked as if she were following a plow, and her stout legs made sharp crops at the ground. She went through the hedge and down the trail

[97]

that led to the outbilly, and there she kicked the door closed as she passed.

When she was out of sight Uncle Harry switched his chair around. Lifting his leg, he drew a match the full length of his thigh, and near the knee it exploded, leaving a yellowish stain. "If I'd known," he said, "I could've finished up that grain——"

"You haven't so much as asked," said Aunt Sarah, "if he was plannin' to stay."

"Of course he's stayin'," said Uncle Harry. "If he ain't stayin', why'd he be comin'?"

"Maybe he's seen enough as it is."

"Maybe he's seen enough," said Uncle Harry, "but it ain't enough for me. I come a little more than eight miles and left my grain just settin'——"

"If I was him," said Aunt Sarah, "I'd want to be where it was cool. Hasn't been cool here since you cut my tree."

"That tree was dead—the man said it was dead."

"It was green an shady—no more dead than you an me."

"Ain't that dead enough?"

"Well—" said Aunt Sarah, and walked to stand at the screen.

"Only difference is," said Uncle Harry, "there's no one to cut us down. Nobody from the W.P.A. to look at your tongue an say, 'This one's dead.'"

"Difference is," said Aunt Sarah, "nobody around to haul it away. Roy with a girl soon to be a lady and all the rest of us good as dead. The trees and the rest of us good as dead." Aunt Sarah turned and they looked at each other, mildly, blankly—then she said, "You bring my flour?"

"No, I guess I forgot it—your callin' made me forget it. Left your flour and my grain just settin'—" he said.

From behind the outbilly Agee Ward could see Will's farm. Where the trail opened on the yard one fork went left to the pigsty and the sheds, the other fork made a slow curve toward the house. It had once curved to go by something—now the something was no longer there. The small narrow house sat on a high foundation and, with a porch at each end, looked like a caboose. It had been painted white and then sun-baked soft, like pottery. A new combine, the color of a fire engine, sat in the yard. The exact center of the yard. It had been parked where it neither crowded nor seemed removed from the house, and where it might be seen from the kitchen door. A lean, nearly brittle-lean, man looked at it from there. He stood wiping his hands on the long faded tail of his shirt, the cloth soaking dark, then hung to dry at the sag in his bib. The tan at his throat was like a birthmark or a metallic bruise. His straw was off, and the top of his narrow, bird-like head was the color of the house where the clapboards streaked it with shadows like skimmed milk. He had neither the chest, the hands, nor the bottom of the Ward line. His overalls hung as empty as Aunt Sarah's dress, drooping straight from his shoulders to where the cuffs were like earth banked around two poles. At the top of the steps Agee Ward turned and looked where Will seemed to be looking.

"Ain't she a beauty?" said Will.

"You bet," he said, and looked at the bright red enamel on the combine. Will opened the screen and came out beside him. He raised the front tail of his shirt, wiped his face, and then looked at the stain on the cloth. He let it drop and rubbed his hands on the front of his bib.

"Well, how you people been?"

"Fine," he said, "just fine—and how've you been?"

Looking up, blinking, Will said, "Well, we been just fine." They looked out over the yard at his combine, his henhouse, his pigsty, and three new bright red sheds. A power line crossed from the house to the sty and somewhere behind a motor pumped water.

"You grown some," said Will.

"Some—" he said.

In the house Adaline was saying, "Cally May, now if you'll go an fetch the men——"

Then they turned and Cally May was standing, her nails snapping, at the screen.

Combine dust, the color of meal, floated on the water while he washed his hands. He carried the pan to the screen and emptied it where Leghorn pullets scratched. Cally May brought him a towel and as he wiped his hands the word GOLD, then MEDAL appeared. He wiped his face and after a moment, faintly, the word FLOUR. Adaline was saying that in four, five years all Mother Sarah talked about was her tree.

"Well, she planted it," said Will.

"But it *was* dead," said Adaline. Then she said, "Cally May, now you show Mr. Ward where he's to sit down." Cally May walked to the table and stood behind a chair. Her new dress had a white satin bow with lace at the throat and lace trim at the sleeves. But it still wasn't quite new enough to cover her knees.

"Thank you very much," he said, and Cally May walked away, staring happily. She stood at the screen, her knees and toes pressed together.

"Cally May," said Adaline, "if you'll just bring the iced tea. No," she said, "I'll get it—you keep Mr. Ward company." At the door to her electric icebox she said, "I just wonder sometimes what I did without it—how the milk and butter ever did without it."

"It ain't paid for yet," said Will.

"It's payin' for itself," she said. With her hand on the lift she stood looking at it.

"We got power through here now—Nebraska power," Will said.

"And three cows," Adaline said. "Seems all I do is make ice cream. Now I hope you like ice cream?"

"Who ever heard," said Will, "of not likin' ice cream?"

Adaline held up a tray of what seemed to be butter. "This time of year it's like butter—in the winter it's just plain white. In the winter it looks like olie margerine."

"Something in fresh grass," said Will, "makes it yellow. I read that it's grass that makes swiss cheese swiss. Can't grow grass just like that over here."

"All he does all winter long is set an read. He's as good as Cally May for likin' to read. Cally May's read every single book in her school."

Cally May sat down, stood up, sat down.

"Now you all sit right down," Adaline said.

"The folks got one too," said Will, looking at the refriger-ator.

"But they don't know what it's for. They won't learn to

eat what it is you need it for. I never seen but eggs and milk in it," she said.

"She's too old to start learnin'," said Will.

"An run the farm."

"An run the farm."

"While she could get out an run it, it was *run*—neat as a pin."

"Well—" said Will. "We eat now?"

"While it's good an hot," she said. As Will reached for the potatoes, "Mind your napkin now," she said. "I always have to tell him that. You'd think he didn't know what it's for." As she helped herself to the peas she said, "We don't say grace much any more. It isn't that we're disrespectful——"

"We just don't say it," Will said.

"When you've had ten years like we've had it, you come to rely on yourself," she said. "Cally May, you asked Mr. Ward if he takes sugar in his tea?"

They ate boiled potatoes, meat in a stew, and peas in a thick cream sauce. Sometimes they looked up to drink their iced tea, or looked through the door at the yard and the combine. Sometimes a pullet came up to the screen, cocked its head, and peered in. Once Adaline said, "Cally May!" and Cally May wiped her nose. Then they ate the yellow ice cream in saucers, silently, except for their spoons.

Pushing back his chair, looking for his napkin, Will found it far inside of his bib. He left it there and reached for a toothpick—then put it back, and passed the box around.

"I drove right by," Agee said, "looking for the trees."

"When you come by again we'll have some more," Will said.

"You planting trees?"

"Always planting trees. The thing about Dad," said Will, "is how he planted trees. I guess he put in maybe thirty thousand trees. When he came out there wasn't a tree."

"Like Lone Tree," he said.

"Sure," said Will, "like Lone Tree."

"An then they'll die in a drouth," said Adaline. "An then they'll have to be planted again."

"He ain't a farmer," Will said, "who thinks what he plants ain't liable to die." He walked over and took his straw from the door, dropped his toothpick in the cob box.

"Then there ain't many farmers," said Adaline.

"No," said Will, "I guess there ain't."

Cally May took an apron from behind the door and Adaline helped her put it on. Will opened the screen, and as it creaked and slammed behind him there was a noise like a stampede or a drunken brawl in the yard, and in a wild shrill chorus the pigs squealed.

A breeze came up, sounding the curtains and waving the bow on Cally May's dress. "While we're cleanin' up here why don't you just look around a bit?" Adaline said. "It's cooler out than in now—it's cool in the yard."

But when he opened the screen a huge, powder-blue cat sidled into the kitchen. He was the size of a small dog with a dusty, smoky softness as if he had just been singed. "Holy—" he said, then, "What a cat!"

"All the rest was spotted," Adaline said, "or with pretty markin's, but Moses is just plain."

"Moses?" he said.

"Father Ward named him Moses. When he was a little one with nothin' to do the rest was always followin' him places."

"MeeeowooOOOWEEEeeeEH!" said Moses. At the tip of his ears the blue fuzz was pearl gray, but he glowed all over as if powdered with glass. Cally May put down her dish towel and scooped him up. He neither liked nor disliked it; he just let himself sag.

"Cally May!" said Adaline, and Cally May put him down.

"Kitty-kitty," said Cally May.

"There's always chores to do," said Adaline, "but soon as Will's through we'll come by for a minute before you folks go to bed. I suppose you're tired?"

"No," he said.

"Well, I'm always ready for bed. Soon as it's dark there's no other place I'd rather be."

As he opened the screen he could hear Aunt Sarah calling her chickens, and when she stopped he could hear some of them flapping their wings.

"For the longest time," Adaline said, "our chickens would try to get in on that too. We had the awfulest time until the old ones died and the young ones learned to know better. Now they know that by running over there all they do is miss better stuff here."

Two horses stood at the fence, the mare with blind, opaque blue eyes. In the steady drone of flies their hides quivered like the surface of water—the mare lifted her head, shied away from his steps in the grass. Wading through the tangle of shrubs he stopped to wipe his face clean of cobwebs, and heard the leaves brushed by something following him. An old dog was dragging along, head down. He was rheumatic, and his front legs towed his rear legs along, his matted dung-heavy tail raking the leaves. At his feet the dog stopped and sniffed the legs of his pants. "Well—" he said, and the old dog's tail lifted a bit, then settled again in the leaves. They stood there, waiting, then together they went on.

They stopped at the barn and looked in. In the lean-to for twenty-five cows stood a taffy-colored Guernsey with a half dozen spotted cats sitting around. A pair of yellow eyes blinked in the feed box, then blinked away. The sudsy squirt of milk beat time in the pail. It skipped a beat—and through the legs of the Guernsey a sharp white stream splashed the row of cats. All but one caught it expertly, full in the face, but the last one stood up and stopped it with her frame. Then she sat down and slowly licked herself clean.

"She's half blind," said Uncle Harry, "but she ain't too blind to lick it off." Behind the spotted cats several kittens climbed around, licked up what the others had missed. Coming out with the pail, Uncle Harry said, "Where you find Shorty?" and looked down at the dog.

"I didn't," he said. "Shorty found me."

"His legs always been too close to the ground. He's an old man—he's old as Cally May."

"He's hot," said Agee Ward. "Think he'd like to be clipped."

"No sir-ree!" said Uncle Harry. "Time we clipped him he didn't like it at all. We had three dogs then and he wouldn't come an eat until the other dogs walked away. Think he knew he looked even funnier yet without his pants."

They walked along single file toward the house. There was a light in the kitchen and he could see Aunt Sarah cleaning off

the eggs. "He's been a good dog," Uncle Harry went on—
"Think what he misses most now is the herd. Could send him
out alone any time and he'd bring 'em all in. Cow I got now
comes in by herself—think it always makes him pretty
mad."

Aunt Sarah came to the screen with some eggs still in her
apron. "There's one more settin' in the cobhouse," she said.
Uncle Harry stopped, put down the pail. The cats curled their
tails over the rim and leaned on the sides, rubbing against the
handle wire.

"Funny," said Uncle Harry, "how them chickens know
they got more use for them eggs right now than we have."

"Nothin' funny," said Aunt Sarah. "I'm just too old an
tired to look."

Uncle Harry shooed the cats away and picked up the pail.
Scooping a handful of foam from the top, he stretched his
fingers to the kittens, one for each of them, and they cleaned
his hand to the wrist. As he wiped his fingers on his overalls,
Aunt Sarah turned and walked away. Uncle Harry followed
her in with the pail. There was a clucking in the cobhouse,
then the henhouse, and when Agee Ward turned to speak
to Shorty he saw that this was the word that the chickens were
passing along.

Aunt Sarah said, "Why don't you come in where it's light?"
She lay on the couch near the window, her teeth resting on
the sill, and her glass eye in the upper plate's red palm, looking out at him. Lumpy with flies, a cord suspended a small
yellow bulb from the ceiling. The single, looping wire vibrated
from some electric motor, then glowed bright and certain as

the refrigerator shut off. Aunt Sarah's refrigerator sat in front of a door. The brass doorknob had been removed, and now filled the toe of a sock stretched beside her, the bolt neck sticking through the hole. Aunt Sarah lay flat, the thickness of a comfort, and nearly as smooth. With a newspaper she fanned the air over her face, her mouth open, her long narrow feet up stiff and straight.

"You get enough to eat?" she said.

"Too much," he said. "I ate too much."

She moved as if she would look to see—then changed her mind. The three straight chairs had been returned to their places at the wall. Everything spaced, evenly spaced, the chairs, the table, the icebox, the couch—everything with its own proper identity. A faded photograph had a proper frame of space on the wall. There were no *arrangements,* no groupings of any kind. Things were themselves and not one of a group of things. Nothing was done to make it look more, or to make it look less than what it was. Where the piano had been the space remained unoccupied. The wallpaper flowers were still in season and the trailing fern leaves were still spring green. Where the rug had been the floor was painted brown. Bits of frayed rug, like mop droppings, caulked the cracks. Where Aunt Sarah walked her shoes the floor was dull and faded, but where she walked in her stockings it had a high shine. Somewhere in the yard Cally May laughed and Aunt Sarah stopped her fanning to listen.

"You nice to her?"

"*Her*—?" he said.

"I keep forgettin' that you ain't married." She turned her good eye toward him and said, "There ain't so much time as you think to be nice in. There's more time than you think to sit around waitin'."

Uncle Harry came in with his shoes, his socks stuffed in his side pockets. His long underwear dragged on the floor and his right heel walked on it. "First time I been upstairs," he said, "since the wind blew in the window. Sleep down here now—it's cooler down here."

"While my tree was there," said Aunt Sarah, "we never had trouble sleepin'."

Uncle Harry dropped his shoes and went into the front room after his rocker. He brought it in to the foot of the couch and sat down facing Aunt Sarah. He put his feet up on the end beside hers, nearly touching, his toes wiggling.

"That tree was dead," he said. "Likely fallen on you by now."

"Might as well as go on doin' without it."

"Landsakes!" said Adaline, opening the screen, "you still talkin' about that tree?"

"What's wrong with that?" said Uncle Harry.

"Fifty-two years—" said Aunt Sarah. "That's young for a tree."

"Where's Will?" said Uncle Harry.

"He's comin'," Adaline said. Uncle Harry took his pipe from his pocket, cleaned the bowl. He dropped the ashes in his hand and carefully weeded out the tobacco—he emptied the ashes in his pants cuff, put the tobacco back in his pipe.

"Where's Will?" he said.

"I just told you he was comin'."

Lighting his pipe, Uncle Harry said, "A rain right now would grow the best corn we ever had. High as my head out there right now."

[108]

"The land's coming back," said Agee Ward.

"Back!" said Uncle Harry. "Who said it's been away?"

"It was pretty dry," he said.

"Of course it was dry—always might be dry."

"We never lacked a crop," said Aunt Sarah. "If it wasn't corn there'd be wheat or rye."

"Land comin' back—well, now!" said Uncle Harry. He turned and looked at Sarah, then back at Agee Ward. "What you mean, maybe, is that you come back to the land." He slapped his hand on his leg then waved his hand at the dust. "Land comin' back—well, now," he said. "Never lacked a crop—never borrowed a penny."

Aunt Sarah sat up and looked out with one eye. "It was thin a spell—but except for my trees I don't think I'd remarked it."

"Right then," said Uncle Harry, "could've sold it for cash. A city fellow come around an offered me cash. Offered me just twice what it cost me—in cash."

"He come out an snooped around," said Aunt Sarah. "If I hadn't been so sick right then with my eye——"

"I planned to shoot him," said Uncle Harry, "but doggone he didn't come back. I guess it scared him just as bad what I said about my trees. I said in fifty years I'd planted forty thousand trees and I reckoned the dead ones at about thirty dollars apiece. The live ones, I said, would run a little more."

"Only thing that really hurt—" said Aunt Sarah, and sat up. She wet her lips but she didn't say anything.

"You city men ought to come back oftener," said Uncle Harry.

"Now," said Aunt Sarah, "he ain't so bad. You're forgettin' he's a Ward just the same as you."

"When a man talks about the land comin' back you know it's him that's been away."

"Hear you talk," said Aunt Sarah, "you'd think it was him that cut my tree."

"I declare!" said Adaline. "If I hear mention of that tree once more I'm goin' home. And if I was Mr. Ward I'd think a long time before comin' again."

"If he don't come oftener," Uncle Harry said, "he won't know a live tree from a dead one. Same as some other people I know."

Adaline got up and started toward the door but as she reached the screen Cally May came in. "Cally May," she said, "you go tell your Daddy that he just needn't bother. You tell him that your Mother is right this minute on her way home."

Although Cally May stopped in the door to hear this, she didn't seem to be listening. And when her mother stopped talking she walked past her into the room. She was holding something in her arms, cuddling it like a doll or a baby, but until she stood beneath the light they couldn't see what it was. It was Moses—but not as passive as he first had been. He now refused to lie on his back and Cally May had to let most of him sag. She stood with him facing Uncle Harry, who sat up and rubbed his eyes. Turning from her, Uncle Harry looked at each one of them as if to make sure they were there.

"What—" he said, "what's got in her? I never seen her holdin' up a cat."

Adaline came back in and Uncle Harry looked at her. Cally May turned away from him and held up Moses for Agee Ward. She was so happy she could hardly stand it, her mouth hung open, and her eyes rolled.

"She's a beauty!" said Agee Ward.

"Ain't that a Tom?" said Uncle Harry. "Or is he talkin' about Cally May?" Cally May held him higher and Moses was very much a Tom. "What's got in her?" said Uncle Harry.

"Ain't you ever liked a thing?" said Aunt Sarah. "Ain't you ever liked a thing enough to hug it?"

"She feelin' all right?" said Uncle Harry.

"Cally May," said Adaline, "you'll make him sick. It's holdin' cats like that that makes 'em sick." Cally May stooped low, her knees cracking, and let Moses try his legs. He stood a moment, skeptical, then he walked away. On her hands and knees Cally May followed him.

"Will tinkerin' with that dam machine?" said Uncle Harry.

"He takes the same care of his machine he does with a horse," said Adaline. "He wouldn't think of goin' to bed without oilin' the one an' feedin' the other. He wouldn't think of lettin' either one go to seed."

Cally May and Moses entered again, crossed through the light. The house seemed to be new to Moses and he made a tour, Cally May right behind.

"I swear—!" said Uncle Harry. "She all right?"

"Cally May!" said Adaline. "You stop hecklin' him."

"Whoever heard," said Aunt Sarah, "that huggin' is hecklin'?"

Getting up from his chair, Agee Ward crossed to the wall, bent over to look at the framed photograph. It was so faded that he hadn't even recognized it. There they were—all the Wards—all lined up near Zanesville, ten men and two ladies in the snow. "This picture," he said, "I've got one of these too."

[111]

"I was first," said Uncle Harry, "and now I'm the last."

"I never learned them all," he said. "Who are the young ones?"

"Lookin' alike?"

"Yes," he said.

"Alfonso and Lorenzo—they was twins."

"*Alfonso* Ward?" he said.

"They come so late," said Uncle Harry, "guess the folks run out of names. Take back, back in—say on there about when it was?"

"Eighteen-ninety-two," he said.

"Bring me that thing!" said Uncle Harry. Agee Ward unhooked it from the nail and brought it over. "Lord—it's fadin'!"

"You wearin' your glasses?" Adaline said.

"Maybe that's it," said Uncle Harry. Then he looked up and said, "Come to think, they never had faces. Been forty years since they had any faces." From the front room Adaline brought him his glasses. He moved them up and down his nose until he got the right focus. "Think it's worse,"·he said. "Think it has been fadin'——"

"Everybody dead, think it would be fadin'. Same," said Aunt Sarah, "as you an' me are fadin'."

"Come to think," said Uncle Harry, "never did know their faces. Think I more or less knew 'em from how they were standin'. Now there," he said, pointing, "standin' there is Mitchell. Just died"—he turned and pointed straight east through the window—"died right over there, just south of Sioux City. Your Aunt May," he said, pointing south, "in Falls City."

[112]

"She has three the nicest boys, all in Lincoln," said Aunt Sarah.

"All the boys had girls, an all the girls had boys! Not a Ward among them!" said Uncle Harry.

"Them boys is all Ward."

"But their name is O'Connell." Uncle Harry shook his head and looked back at the picture. "Out in Cozad—" he went on, but first hitched around his chair. Pointing out through the kitchen, past the cobhouse, he said, "Last time I saw Emerson he was as spry as a kid."

"He had pictures on the wall he hand-painted," said Aunt Sarah.

"One of a dog," said Uncle Harry. "You'd swear he'd come right down an bite you."

"An now he's gone," Aunt Sarah said.

"All around," said Uncle Harry, "we're fertilizin' all around."

"We ain't all," said Aunt Sarah.

"We took a lot out," Uncle Harry said, "but now we're puttin' all of it back." He raised his hand, the fingers spread. "Alfonso—Lorenzo—Martha—Mitchell—May—" He raised his other hand. "Luther—Paul—Emerson—Henry—an . . ."

"Bryan—" said Aunt Sarah.

"An William," he said. "Now who else?"

"You," said Adaline.

"I ain't dead yet," said Uncle Harry.

"Kermit—?" said Agee Ward.

"We just ain't heard—we ain't heard sure," said Aunt Sarah.

"He was a maverick," said Uncle Harry, "but I reckon he's dead." He pushed his glasses back and squinted at the photograph. "Dang," he said, "I just noticed how little we were lookin' alike." He put the picture down in his lap and rubbed at his eyes.

"Ain't Will comin'?" Aunt Sarah said.

"I guess he ain't," Adaline said. "He's been havin' trouble with that new chick feeder an you know how he is."

"I know," Aunt Sarah said.

"Cally May," said Adaline, "pick yourself up now for we're goin' home." Back in the corner Cally May scooped up Moses and then let him sag. Uncle Harry put his glasses back in the case.

"I seen the sheets on the front bed," said Uncle Harry. "Hand embroidery on the pillow."

"Oh, my!" said Adaline.

"I'm sick an tired of savin' 'em," said Aunt Sarah.

At the door Adaline said, "You'll be leavin' after breakfast?"

"I guess so," said Agee Ward.

"Where's Will?" said Uncle Harry.

"Cally May," said Adaline, "now you come along."

"I want to thank you for the fine supper," said Agee Ward.

"Except for the sauce on the peas," said Adaline, "there wasn't anything that was at all special. With the berries gone there ain't much to offer special."

"Think of him tinkerin' with that dam machine when there's people come a hundred miles to see him."

Adaline opened her mouth, then closed it, pushed on the screen. Cally May followed her out, with Moses still sagging, and as they crossed the yard Adaline said, "Cally May, you

[114]

put him down before he goes sick all over you—all over your new dress and your new bow."

In the kitchen Agee Ward took a drink and then let the dipper float. It was quiet in the house, but at the screen the night seemed a huge bottle of insects and he stepped back as if the lid might fly off. Coming back toward the light, he saw that Aunt Sarah was asleep. The newspaper fan now lay on her face, the fingers of one hand slowly opening. Uncle Harry was looking at the photograph in his lap. In his left hand he held his watch, the back of the case snapped open, and with his right, absently, he poked around with the key. "Dang!" he said, and held it up to find the keyhole, began to wind.

*When he was a kid he saw the town through a
crack in the grain elevator, an island of trees in the
quiet sea of corn. That had been the day the end of
the world was at hand. Miss Baumgartner let them
out of school so they could go and watch it end, or
hide and peek at it from somewhere. Dean Cole and
him walked a block and then they ran. They ran all
the way to the tracks and down the tracks to the
grain elevator, through a hole in the bottom and up
the ladder inside. They stretched on their bellies and
looked through a crack at the town. They could see
all the way to Chapman and a train smoking somewhere. They could see the Platte beyond the tall corn
and the bridge where Peewee had dived in the sand,
and they could see T. B. Horde driving his county
fair mare. They could see it all and the end of the
world was at hand.*

The end of the world! he said.

HOO-RAY! said Dean Cole.

ON THE EVENING SIDE OF THE
street men left their cars parked, and their women, then
crossed to stand on the curbing and face into the sun. The

old men rocked stiffly, their knees cocked, flexing their bib straps, stropping their hooked thumbs softly up and down. The young men smoothed the brim of their straws and looked down their denim fronts to the fly. They stared at their feet and the button shadows ironed on the fly.

In Eddie Cahow's barber shop two of the three chairs were empty but a small boy sat high and quiet in the third. Eddie Cahow had just finished with his hair. The air was dusty and sparking with the sweet-smelling powder and the boy stared at his new face in the mirror. The pin-striped cloth sloped from his ears to the cushioned board crossed on the chair arms, and his bare feet, the toes wiggling, were placed on the seat. Eddie Cahow gave him four shots of the pea-green water, then one more on the cow lick that popped in the rear.

At the corner Agee Ward turned right and faced the tracks. The warning bell began to ring, and rising from his chair in the signal tower a man with a Pillsbury flour hat cranked down the gates. As they settled, bobbing, the Streamliner honked to the east. A block the other side of the tracks an old man drew in his mare, set the whip in the stock, and braced his feet on the board. He tacked a bit with the reins until the mare turned away from the honking, then he sat straight, his knees spread, ready for anything.

The train went through, the gates went up, and as the dust settled the old man raised his voice, spoke to her. Together they relaxed, and then she pulled him into town.

The street beyond had cement gutters where there had been grass. Riding sidesaddle, one leg through the bar, a boy went by on a Ranger bicycle, the stand dragging and marbles rattling in the tool box. His left pants leg was rolled and a smear of chain grease went around his bare leg. Strips of thin berrybasket wood, fastened to the frame, buzzed against the spokes, and as he coasted he blew on a rubber schnozzle that drooped from his mouth. Where the elms hung low and made him duck he said, "Whoops—low ceiling!" and then, with his throttle open, crossed the tracks.

A woman in a bonnet and a clothespin apron was taking down wash. She liked the feel of the bag full of clothespins and dipped her hands into them like grain. Over a sheet blue with rinse and leaf shadows she watched him go by.

> *In the summer he would sit on the steps where there were ants and the shadows moved, or on the culvert waiting for garter snakes. Or he would drag the rake in the ditch grass shooing at them. He would let grasshoppers spit in his hand and rub the juice in his hair for luck and pick the soft tar out of the sidewalk with his teeth. He would do that with Dean Cole looking at him. Dean Cole would do something else and he would look. He would watch Dean Cole lie on his face while forty-two freight cars went over him—and then Dean Cole would watch him eat a cow pie. Dean Cole would jump up and down and yell, but he knew he won. He won, for it's nothing to eat a cow pie like it is to see someone run over, and the best thing to be run over by was a train. And Dean Cole knew it for he would stop yelling and just look at him. He would just stare until he had finished with his cow pie.*

Dean Cole's house had been something like yellow—it still was. There was a scar between the small windows where the front porch had been, and a spare tire was used as a flower box in the yard. Four sunflowers, roof high, grew from it. Over the door license plates were arranged chronologically, beginning with Alabama 1917. A dog stood at the screen, his eyes softly closed, sniffing, and when a boy yelled somewhere he wagged his tail.

Grass spread the loose boards in Mrs. Riddlemosher's walk. A rocker with a patch-quilt seat sat on the back porch. Loose pages of a comic book were spread about in the yard and a small boy with a rubber-band pistol stood at the screen. He was chewing the barrel, pensively, and listening to the Chesterfield Hour. Someone crossed through the room and the music went off, the news came on, and the boy turned, his mouth open—then pushed the gun back in. Closing his eyes, he went on chewing it.

Through the vines was Eoff's grocery store and a brown dog drinking at the fountain. Sparrows dropped from the trees to the wires and then from the wires to the ditch grass. A pigeon dropped from the belfry to the barn. He walked along the tin roof to the henhouse, looked inside. Jewel's Tea Wagon crossed the tracks and the dust came up and went by. More sparrows dropped from the wires and stirred the grass near the road. Mrs. Riddlemosher stopped picking currants and turned with her pan. Mrs. Mulhauser came and stood at the screen. Tipping her sunbonnet back, Mrs. Riddlemosher looked toward the square where the dust came marching down the road with the rain.

The house with the cupola and run-around porch had been painted, the porch glassed in, but the fence at the bottom still ran-around. There were still three birch trees in the yard. A dog got up from the lawn and followed him. When the dog saw he didn't know where he was going he took the lead, and led toward the bridge. There were still cracks—but there was no water below.

> When there was no water below he would walk and stand in the corn. He would do something if the leaves were too quiet or he would yell when somebody went by. Or he would go where sick people went and the cottonwoods snowed. Or he would lie on his face and spit through a crack in the bridge. Sometimes it looked as far as the sky up or a well down. Sometimes it looked a boat, a bird, or a cloud drifting away. Sometimes it was the sky dirty-upside-down and raining brown weeds. And sometimes it was mirror, mirror there on the wall.

The dog came out of the cornfield, sneezing, and led him back across the bridge. They took the street with a fine row of telephone poles. He could feel the hum in the wires on the fence and he could see it on the pool in the ditch grass. When he closed his eyes he could feel and hear it at the same time. When he opened them they were passing the Chautauqua grounds.

> Across the road was the short grass and the meadow. Beyond the meadow was the long grass and the tree. Where the grass was short the Carnival came and where it was long came the Chautauqua. Where it was yellow with sawdust the circus came. Beyond that were the buckboard seats in the weeds. After the Circus, the Carnival, the Chautauqua, came the boys. After the buggies were gone and the

lights out came the girls. The big boys and the girls.
And after the girls came the little boys and the weeds.

Beyond the square a row of stores faced the sun like an execution, a row of stubborn old men lined up to be shot. Over the door of the first was a Coca-Cola sign. As he opened the screen a cowbell jangled in the back of the store, and the three people seated at the counter looked at him. They were eating three different-colored sodas, very slowly, with a spoon. They wore stiff, brightly-varnished straw hats and as they stopped spooning, raised their heads, he could see that they shared the same face. But the one in the center had weathered—something—and these were her twins. They were now the same size and all looked through their eyes the same. A big, pleasant woman was wiping the counter and the knobs of the flavor labels, and as she dropped the rag she smiled and said, "Coke?"

"Please," he said.

"Cherry?"

"Well—"

"It's popular," she said. "I make more cherry cokes than any. Hot days like this I make a dozen cherry cokes a day."

"Well—" he said.

"I do," she said, and made him a cherry coke.

Harness and straps of black leather hung from hooks in the ceiling, and horse collars were like empty picture frames along the wall. The dry goods and hardware were in the rear. A man in faded red suspenders and long fleece-lined underwear was rolling up a bolt of flowered cloth. The sleeves of his underwear and the backs of his hands were powdered with a fine yellow meal. After folding the cloth he picked up a flour scoop and went out the rear door. A draft of wet mash and stale baled hay came up and went by.

"Maybe I put too much cherry?" she said.

"No," he said. "No—it's just fine."

"I like to make the first one strong," she said. "Better a little strong than a little weak."

"You bet," he said. She smiled at him, wiping the counter, so he said, "Ward—you ever know a Henry Ward?"

"He was a nice boy."

"He was—"

"Rode in a gig with him to Chapman—think he married a Chapman girl." He looked at her and she turned to the three women at the counter. "Mrs. Blake," she said, "how big were you back in nine and ten?"

"I was born in ninety-nine, Mrs. Canby," she said.

"You was a little tyke then?"

"I never was big—all us Macys is small." She looked at her twins, the left one, then the right one.

"Your Daddy," said Mrs. Canby, "was a pretty big man."

"He was a Hoskins," she said. "He wasn't a Macy at all."

"He was a fine big man."

"The Hoskins is big. The Hoskins live big and the Macys live long."

"Your boy Roy is a Hoskins."

"My girls is Macys," she said. The girls looked at her and at each other, solemnly. They were as slight as grass with over-size heads, their wide-brimmed straws like the seed flowering.

"You was such a little tyke," said Mrs. Canby, "you likely don't remember him."

Turning to him, Mrs. Blake said, "You his boy?"

"Yes," he said.

"Like my girls is mine, I'd say you're hers," she said.

"You saw her?"

"No—I'd just say so." She finished her soda and put the spoon in the glass. In the mirror she looked at the three Macys as one.

"Oh, Frank!" Mrs. Canby called.

"Coming," said Frank. He came up from the back with the flour scoop in his hand and stood blinking at her.

"Frank," she said, "you remember Henry Ward?"

"Yes, I do."

"Well—who'd he marry? She was a Chapman girl—but who?"

Mr. Canby tipped the scoop up and down and stared into it. The sleeves of his underwear were rolled and his arms were whiter than the fleece lining.

"We was envious," he said, "that's all I remember. There wasn't a man in Merrick County that wasn't envious."

"An you don't remember her?"

"What her name was, I don't."

"Ain't that a man now, Mrs. Blake?" said Mrs. Canby.

Mrs. Blake shook her head as if it certainly was. She backed off the stool and her twins put down their sodas, also backed off. They stood about an inch higher, but they were not taller, merely not yet bent. They stood one on each side of her as she said—"The Blakes and Hoskins even forgot where they was from."

"Where was they from?" said Mrs. Canby.

"They forgot," Mrs. Blake said. She looked at her Macy

twins and they pulled their straw hats down. "There's Macys in South Carolina and then there's Macys where we're from. Lou Belle," she said, turning, "where is your Macy people from?"

"Murfreesboro," said Lou Belle. The other girl nodded and they both looked at Mrs. Blake.

"I've been through there," he said, to say something.

"I've never been back," said Mrs. Blake. She looked through the window as if Murfreesboro were there, then she pushed on the screen and walked out. The twins were behind her before the screen had closed. They walked single file across the tracks and then across a field to where a cow was tethered.

"You ask Eddie Cahow?" Mr. Canby said.

"The barber?"

"He can tell you who you are by just trimmin' your head. Accordin' to Eddie, he can tell you what's inside of it too."

"I think he's busy right now," said Agee Ward.

"That don't mean a thing. Nothin' he likes to do more than clean his comb and talk a spell."

Mrs. Canby said, "He'd be like to know. If she was raised around here, he'd be the one to know."

"Nothin' he'd like more than to talk to you."

Agee Ward left a nickel on the counter and went out in the street. In the windshield of a parked car he could see that Eddie Cahow was still busy, but not so busy that he hadn't noticed him. Over the head of the man in the chair Eddie Cahow snapped his shears like castanets. Agee Ward turned to look at two posters propped up in his window. One of them advertised daring motorcycle races and a hill-climbing contest for cash prizes. The second advertised KING KONG, with a portrait, now showing at the Empress. Through the screen he could hear the crickety-chirping of Eddie Cahow's shears. As he looked up, as if to see what *that* was, Eddie Cahow smiled and waved his comb at him.

"Why don't you step in?" Eddie Cahow said, and nodded at the screen. Agee Ward opened it and stepped inside. There was a long bench against the wall and three wire-back chairs covered with magazines.

"Mr. Cahow——" he said.

"You be quiet," said Eddie Cahow. "You be quiet a minute and I'll tell you who you are." He stopped trimming hair and looked at Agee Ward in the mirror. He blew the hair from his comb and tapped it on his sleeve.

"You're Grace an Hank's boy—mostly Grace," he said.

"I guess so——"

"They call you Dwight?"

"Fayette——" he said, "Fayette Agee Ward."

"Oh sure—your little brother. Now I'd near forgotten him."

"Little brother?" he said.

"Your little brother Fayette. Named him after brother of her own who died. Poor little fella only lived a few months."

"My brother?" he repeated.

"Buried right over there." Eddie Cahow pointed with his shears to the south. "Right along with your mother, grandmother, an such."

He sat down on the bench and looked at Eddie Cahow. Eddie Cahow tipped the man's head a bit, combed down the hair.

"Yes, sir!" said Eddie Cahow. "When I saw you I said, 'Eddie Cahow, there goes two, three people that you know.'

You bet, and sure enough!" He looked up, chirping his shears. "You married?"

"No," he said.

"Is there issue from that union?"

"I'm not married—yet," he said.

"Oh—" said Eddie Cahow, "so you're not married."

"No."

Eddie Cahow thought about that, then he tapped the head of the man in the chair. "Mr. Applegate," he said, "you remember that Ward boy?"

Mr. Applegate turned and looked at Agee Ward. His face was a weathered leathery tan but with his new haircut he looked scalped.

"He the one went to Californy?"

"No—" said Agee Ward, "I don't think so."

"Yes, that's right," said Eddie Cahow, "on their honeymoon. Went on their honeymoon. Your Daddy was station agent here an they both got passes. Two-way passes."

"I remember him," Mr. Applegate said. He continued to stare at Agee Ward until Eddie Cahow revolved the chair, facing Mr. Applegate back to the mirror again. "I remember him," Mr. Applegate repeated, and closed his eyes.

He kept them closed while Eddie Cahow rubbed his head. There was a ridge worn at the back, coffee-colored from the band of his hat, and the crease appeared up front again over his eyes. At the edge of his mouth tobacco juice began to ooze. He kept his eyes and his mouth shut tight until Eddie Cahow reached for his comb, then he leaned forward, spat, and rocked the last of three spittoons. Leaning back, he closed his eyes while Eddie Cahow combed his hair.

"She sat right there—" said Eddie Cahow, "where you're sittin'. No—no she didn't either, she sat over there where she could sit and look out. And if you're out you tend to see in pretty well right there." He looked up at the mirror, winking, "And was she smart? Smart as she was pretty!"

Mr. Applegate raised his chin and Eddie Cahow unpinned the cloth. He shook the hair out on the floor while Mr. Applegate looked at his new head, front and side, then wiped the juice streak off his chin. Standing up, he wiped his hand on the seat of his pants. They were dark in the seat but fading light on the calves and thighs, and his watch made a pale full moon in his bib. He faced the mirror to put his town straw on, level, with both hands.

"Mr. Applegate," said Eddie Cahow, "you remember them Osborn girls?"

"I was courtin' then," said Mr. Applegate.

"You remember Grace?" said Eddie Cahow. "Now she was the one—you remember her?"

"I was courtin' then—" said Mr. Applegate. They waited for him to go on but he turned and put his right hand into his pocket. He took out a coin purse with brass stud clips and, opening his left hand, spilled out the small change. He put a quarter, a dime, and a nickel in Eddie Cahow's palm. Three two-penny nails he left out and put in the side pocket of his pants.

"And I thank you," Eddie Cahow said.

"I was courtin' about then," he said.

"First thing they did was go to Frisco and make her sick on a boat ride they had."

Mr. Applegate stood at the screen and looked out at a

passing freight. When the man on the caboose waved his hand Mr. Applegate nodded his head. Then he opened the screen and walked to the left.

"Glory me, I'm a fool!" said Eddie Cahow. "Now that I think, it was *her* he was courtin'. Eddie Cahow," he said, "you prate like a fool."

Then he said, "On the other hand, I was right in there myself. If I'd had my way your Daddy wouldn't be dead. B-O-Y BOY!" he said, and slapped his hand on the chair. Then he sat himself in it and cranked it around to face the street.

"You comin' back—or passin' through?" said Eddie Cahow.

"Passin' through," he said.

"And you're not married?"

"No," he said.

Eddie Cahow got up from the chair and began to sweep up the hair. Then he left it in a pile and sat down in the chair again.

"I don't know," said Eddie Cahow, "what it's comin' to. It seems to me somebody's got to do it here. If we got to do it while we're here, it seems to me that this is a fine place to do it. What I want to know is what is wrong with doing it here?"

"Doing what?" he said.

"Whatever it is you go some place else to do. If it's got to be done, why not do it here? It seems to me with everybody goin' there soon won't be places to be from. And without places to be from what kind of a world will it be?"

He shook his head.

"Well, I'll tell you. It'll be full of people like yourself without any place to go."

Agee Ward stood up, then sat down again.

"I've thought of going places myself, but I'm the only one left around here who knows for sure where everybody is from. Sure as I left, one of you people would be wantin' to know. If I'm any judge there's sure goin' to be a lot of missin' people around when I'm gone."

"You ought to write it down."

"You write it down," said Eddie Cahow. "You write down for me what it's like to come through a door and have a man you never saw before tell you who you are."

Agee Ward said nothing.

"See here," said Eddie Cahow, and cranked the chair around to face him. "I got a personal interest—and I wonder if you'd mind a personal question?"

"No—" he said.

"When I seen you there in the door I was as sure as God made little apples that I'd seen you there thirty years before. Well, what I'd like to know is—were you there?" Through Eddie Cahow's flecked glasses Agee Ward could see his eyes twinkle, but his lips were not smiling and he sat waiting, staring at him.

"I've been trying to remember," he said.

"I know," said Eddie Cahow, "when I seen you I knew it. When I seen you moonin' up and down I knew it. But you're the first one I ever put the question to. It ain't the kind of question you're free to put to any man." Agee Ward stood up, then turned from the face he saw in the mirror. "To tell God's honest truth," said Eddie Cahow, "it's gettin' so I can't see the difference. I can't see where she leaves off and you begin. When you can't see a difference like that you sometimes wonder if people feel it—or if it makes any difference what they think they feel."

Through the window Agee Ward saw a Ford lift from the street in the Texaco station, two boys and a windblown girl in the front seat. They waved and peered out as from a rising balloon.

"If Methuselah had a barber shop," said Eddie Cahow, "and lived in a land where nobody moved away, and where the boys and girls got married and had babies, and if I was Methuselah—wouldn't I find myself trimmin' the same head every twenty years? And after two, three hundred years wouldn't I think it was the same man, no matter who it was that walked in with the head?"

"But I moved away," said Agee Ward, "and when you move away what happens to it?"

"Where you're from is where you're goin'," said Eddie Cahow, "and where you're goin' is where you're from."

"Where I'm going is going to be different," he said.

"You say you ain't married?" Eddie Cahow said.

"No."

"If you don't mind *your* p's and q's your goin' places is goin' to stop!" Agee Ward turned away and pushed on the screen. "Don't let them flies in!" said Eddie Cahow, and Agee Ward backed away from the door. Eddie Cahow shooed them out with the barber cloth and stood there looking at the street. Across the square a row of boys waited for the Empress Theatre to open and Mr. Applegate stood reading the display. In the ticket booth a grey-haired woman tipped a green visor over her face and arranged her knitting in her lap. The name of the feature was KING KONG. There were a great many little boys, but the little girls were skeptical and stood at arm's length to look at the pictures of him.

"I want to thank you—" Agee Ward said.

"You need a haircut," said Eddie Cahow, "but now that I think about that head, the hair every which way, I'm goin' to have a bite to eat first." He walked back to the mirror and put his comb and scissors away. Together they walked a block to the right, where the sun came down the road from Chapman, and there Eddie Cahow pinched his arm and walked away.

At the water stack Agee Ward turned south and walked toward a soft swell of ground. There was a steel fence around it and the heavy mesh dulled the shine of the stones, chalk-white and granite, but the high sheen was blurred. As the grass was being cut, the gate was open, a horse unhitched but tethered to the mower. He was wearing a feed bag, and tossing his head to flip the last oats where he could get at them. A canteen in a homemade flannel cooler lay on the ground. Beneath the grass the turf was deep, peat-soft and springy, and when Agee turned he saw the town through the clipped rows of stones. He could see where it had been and where it planned to go. But where it had come, nearly all of it had come, was here at his feet. Here were Muncie—Horde—Blaine—Townsend—Allen—and here was a Cahow. And beyond him Bauman—Newcomb—Fitch—Thorpe—Snider—and Applegate. And on the stone beyond Applegate was the name Ward. It was a large stone of red granite, and it looked new, terribly new, but beneath the name was the date—1910.

ETHEL GRACE WARD
1891–1910
She died so that he might live

Some defect in the stone, and the slanting light, seemed to stress the word *he*. He turned from it and looked at a large, pedestaled stone placed beside it, with the inscription HENRY CLEVELAND WARD. Looking at it, he saw his father standing among the row of brothers, no one so solidly, so well-standing as he. So it was the red granite stood. A long stem of grass waved a shadow over the name, and as he walked past he broke it off. He did not stay to look for anyone else.

At the gate an old man was hitching the horse up to his buggy, a smart little rig with bright red wheels. A round honing stone stuck out of his rear pocket, the center honed in a curve like a handshelling cob. A grass-stained sickle was thrust in his belt.

"Warm—" the old man said.

"Yes," he said. "you bet."

"Some of your people here?"

"In the corner," he said.

"You an Osborn?"

"Ward," he said.

"If she was your mother you're an Osborn!" The old man had raised his voice as if he argued with someone. Now he let it fall and said, "Come over here." As Agee Ward walked over he let the rig slack and looked at him. "Well, now—well, now," he said, and slapped the rump of the mare and straightened the fly net. "Well now—Winona, you ever hear from her?"

"I don't write—much," he said.

"Well now—" he said, and led the mare ahead, then backed her slowly into place. He walked around her, adjusting the harness. "I'm Michael," he said. "When you drop her a line you might just say Michael—say I say hello."

"I'll tell her," he said.

"Be much obliged—" He stayed behind his horse, fooling with the harness, and saying, "Now Dolly—now Dolly, now, now . . ." Over the sway in her back he watched Agee Ward walk away.

The road along the creek had returned to grass, and as he walked the grasshoppers jumped into the light then fell like a quick summer rain in the grain-yellow grass. The sound went ahead of him like brush-fire, and closed in behind. But at the corner of the park the road had been graveled and the side grass mowed. In the bright center of the trees a man held a small boy high for a drink, and the boy cracked at the waist like a sack, his face dipped in the splash. The man was small and had to lean away, his knees bent, as if holding a basket. Another little boy was astride the cannon, whipping it like a horse. The gun carriage was freshly painted red and the barrel and the breech were polished with sitting—and watching the boy ride it away were two little girls. They held each other's hands and were envious, but skeptical. A grown-up girl with long swinging braids walked off alone. In and out of the light and shadow of the trees, past the teeter-totters, the empty swings, past the boy whose eyes were still bright with the long drink he had. Clear across the park to the bandstand and up the steps in the rear to the stage. There—to be sure of it—she stamped twice on the floor. When nothing caved in she walked to the front and clapped her hands. As they came running she tidied her bow, and the boy on the cannon raised one leg, swung side-saddle, but did not dismount. He did not dismount until it was clear that she did not even miss him, would not wait for him, and had already begun to speak. Then he dismounted, a little wildly, and screaming, *Wait!* As he came running she closed her eyes to avoid noticing him and in a low, sweet voice said what she had to say.

On the rise near the tracks Agee Ward stopped to look at the town. To find Lone Tree men came West and planted trees, planted men, planted corn—but the crops of men and corn returned to the East. The paving, the corn, their sons and their daughters went to the East. And in time even the land itself went East. Some of it could be seen, in solution, flowing east toward the Big Muddy, and some of it had been inhaled by the citizens of New York. And yet some of it, some of the best of it, was still here.

He could see that Lone Tree was a house divided, the old town facing the west, but the up-and-coming part of town looking east. For the east was the way out of town, the way to leave. To the east Lone Tree had lengthened like a shadow, but to the west it ended abruptly on the sky. It not merely ended but the sky swept in to invade it, the flood of light and space washing in upon it like a tide. Washing it away, for the square had receded from the blurred fringe of grass and the slats of a fence like fragments of a battered pier. Whatever remained on this edge of town did so at a risk, and a bad one, for only a huddle of old buildings had survived. They faced to the west—a row of old men who had walked to where the sidewalk ended and stood there thinking their thoughts, ignoring this firing squad of light.

The rest of the town looked to the east, the false fronts of the stores like turned-up collars without heads, for the heads had been sucked down. They faced the east—but it was not clear what they seemed to see. But to look at the old men was to turn and face the west, for it was there, out there, that a man still saw something.

As he left the rise the lights came on in the square. They were lights but they cast no shadows, were quiet and framed. The sun leveled down the road from Chapman, entered the town, left it again—but the lights around the square remained in themselves. There was a time in the morning that was the same. But the morning was clear and space had been there to walk upon it—and return upon it—as he had done. He had followed his shadow back, thinking to find himself in the morning—only to find that he was in the evening too. Roads that led out in the morning led back when the lights came on. While there were Osborns there would be, always be, a time in the morning, and while there were evenings there would be the Cahow line. The Uncle Harry-Eddie Cahow line. But the shadow of a man had to pass from morning to evening by going before him—not by lapping at his back. For when he turned, it turned, and the shadow had foreshortened until he stood upon himself, shadowless, here in the street.

APRIL, 1942

THE LAST PHOTOGRAPH IN THE
Album first appeared in the Bel Air *Advance* over the caption MISSING MAN NAMES LOCAL LADY NEAREST KIN. It was
this photograph that Private Reagan came upon on his way
to a funeral—and then continued his journey to see even
stranger things. Originally a four-column feature, it was later
reduced to two columns to illustrate a tribute to Agee Ward
on the back page. This tribute was:

> He brought life
> Into the ,
> Community
> Without marring
> Its beauty.

As there are eighteen men in this picture an arrow is neces-
sary to single out Agee Ward, the life-bringer. Except for the
arrow we might not have noticed him. He stands in the back
row, his clothes are dark, his mouth is shut, and his general
appearance is very dull. When we look at his eyes we see that

[136]

he is not looking out at us. This gives him a negative distinction, as the other seventeen men show more understanding of what a picture is. They are looking out, smiling, knowing that we shall be looking for them—and they are already looking forward to seeing themselves.

Most of these faces might be seen in the background of any news picture—behind a movie star, a murder or surrounding a body lying in the street. All of these men are leaving for War—but in terms of this picture only one of them appears to be going anywhere. This is a boy, or rather a youth, who stands in front of Agee Ward. In this photograph he is not so much a person as a distraction—and Private Reagan was distracted to the point of seeing things. This youth may account for the fact that Agee Ward already seems to be missing, although we have the arrow to prove that he is standing there. The youth hardly comes to Agee Ward's shoulder, he is the smallest man in the group, but it is impossible not to settle on him. To find Agee Ward, to find anybody, we first have to dim this light, put our finger over his face while we look around. But when we lift our finger we see nothing else. Except the fact that we know we have seen this face before.

Private Reagan thought he saw this face in Omaha. Thought he lived with just such a face twenty years ago. But we first saw it in Chicago, standing in front of the Y.M.C.A.—this is the face that we found to be missing. This is the blank in that row of faces reading FEAR—DESIRE—ENVY—and it is still blank, perhaps in order to throw more light. Maybe it is once more that time in the morning when there are lights without shadows—but there will be shadows enough as soon as it is dark.

Seeing this face, citizens of Bel Air stopped doing whatever they were doing long enough to shake their heads, rub their eyes, and ask in a voice loud enough to hear, if there was anything that this Darcy Munger wouldn't do. No—there didn't seem to be anything. But nearly all citizens were agreed that this time he had found his equal—that this time Darcy Munger had found his match. And that whatever it was, the Army would take it out of him.

On the insistence of Peter Spavic, Miss Gussie Newcomb put this picture in the Album—although she thought it a mighty poor likeness of Agee Ward. It was one of those days when he simply didn't look like himself. And standing behind that little Darcy Munger he was a sight! No matter where she started in the picture she ended up with Darcy Munger, who took a mighty good picture for the kind of boy he was. Always wiggling, sniffling, or hopping up and down when she talked to him.

THE ORDEAL OF GUSSIE NEWCOMB

ON THE FIRST WASH DAY IN May Miss Gussie Newcomb of Bel Air was called from her tub to receive a telegram at the front door. As she stood wiping her hands on her apron she could see that the envelope wasn't sealed, and that Mr. Somers already knew what she didn't know.

"I had no idea," he said, "that boy was kin of yours."

"What boy?" Miss Newcomb said.

"That Ward boy," said Mr. Somers, and pointed with his pencil down the drive to her garage. "That boy that lived over your garage for more than a year."

Miss Newcomb stood as if she were trying to remember him. The pods from her Carob tree were all over the walk again and she could see where Mr. Somers had stepped on them. With her broom she stepped out to sweep them off.

"You better read what this says," Mr. Somers said.

Miss Newcomb took the yellow sheet out and read that Agee

Ward 'was reported missing, and that as next of kin she had been notified.

"I never seen that boy," she said, "until he rung the bell right here at my door."

"Now can you beat that!" said Mr. Somers.

"He said he'd heard that I had some nice rooms and I said I had, and that was all to that."

"HMmmmmm—" said Mr. Somers.

"I never butted into his business an he never butted into mine. He was a nice quiet boy—he was all right."

"What you make out of this *kin*?"

"One thing I don't make is gossip," said Miss Newcomb. "All he ever said to me is what I've said to you."

"Sign here," said Mr. Somers.

"When a boy is all alone he might put anything down. Just like them to have rules and make him put something down." Mr. Somers held the pad and Miss Newcomb signed her name. Then she had to erase it for she had written Gussie *Ward*.

"HMMMmmmm—" said Mr. Somers, and started away.

"If you don't mind," said Miss Newcomb, "don't step on my pods." Mr. Somers left the sidewalk and walked in the grass. At the curbing he scraped them off the bottom of his shoes.

"I don't know what to make of it," said Mr. Somers, "but I suppose it's your own business."

"I suppose it is," she said.

"Miss Newcomb," he said, "for all you know maybe that boy was kin of yours—it's getting harder and harder to be sure of some of these things."

Miss Newcomb remembered she had left her clothes boiling on the stove. Then she was standing there in the kitchen, fanning herself, when she thought of something. So Mr. Ward would not send her $18 a month any more? While he was missing he would not have any use for his room, his clothes—or anything. "I'll be back," he said, and of course she thought he would. There was a chair near the door and she sat down to read again—but she had left it, left it in the front room somewhere. After lunch—right after lunch she would air his place out.

At the top of the stairs it was warmer and Miss Newcomb lifted her skirts so that the cool draft from the garage could blow on her legs. For a year she had not done this—not since Agee Ward had moved in, and moved nearly everything that she had in the rooms out. The bed frame along with everything else. What he slept on she didn't know—she had brought him cookies and stood at the door, but not once, not a single time, did he ask her in. He was very nice but she never got past the door. They would stand in the door and talk about his kitty, Cuchulain, which you spelled like that but pronounced another way. Now that he was missing she would never know about him. He was an artist—that was all she really knew. He was an artist—then he was drafted—then he was missing. Half aloud, to herself, Miss Newcomb said, *"Bang-bang-bang!"*

This surprised her so much she dropped her skirts and covered her mouth. Nobody seemed to have heard—the curtain flapped at the hall window, and when it drooped quiet she could hear the bees in the walnut blossoms. Smoothing her skirt, she put the key in the lock and opened the door.

As she always had, she stood a moment peering in. They

would stand there and talk, and though she had the feeling the room was crowded, except for books she was never sure what with. Now, with the door open the room was still so dark that she had to feel her way across it to a window. It was shaded with a pair of pants suspended from the curtain rod. They had not been washed and left to dry; they were just hanging there. They were hanging there for no other reason but to block the light. The room was still a little dark for as bright a day as it was, and she turned to look at the north window. A denim work shirt hung by the sleeves, the long dirty tails pinned to the curtain. This, for the pains she had taken not to have blinds in the room! She sat down on what she hoped was a chair and stared absently. The thought that all of this time, all of last year, he had been sitting up here in the dark, and that she hadn't known it, made her very warm again. The door was still open and she walked out into the hall. Through the hall window she could see Judge Ely tipped over his croquet ball, sighting down the handle of his mallet at the pole across the yard. She turned her head away until she heard him hit the ball. It rolled in and out of the shadows the avocado tree cast on the lawn, and before it stopped the Judge was trailing it.

Miss Newcomb could never understand why an old man, and a judge to boot, couldn't play croquet without having to cheat at it. Pushing his ball instead of hitting it as he should. As he stooped again she saw Reverend Bassett deliberately turn and look away so that he could honestly say he had witnessed no such thing. While she stood there the draft slammed the door to Agee Ward's room. Except for the windows, the pants and shirt, she hadn't really seen one thing—but she felt that she had seen enough for one day. Something about him sitting in the dark that way unnerved her. If she had had any idea that he had come to California to sit in the dark she would have asked him to please sit in it somewhere else. Why did he come out here to do something like that?

While she was wondering, her telephone rang and she got downstairs just in time. It was Evelina Briggs of the Bel Air *Advance*. Was it true, Mrs. Briggs wanted to know, that Miss Newcomb had suffered a loss of kin? Miss Newcomb said that no, it was not. But a dear friend? said Mrs. Briggs. Miss Newcomb said that she supposed that Mr. Ward was her friend, though strictly speaking she was only his landlady. Agee Ward? said Mrs. Briggs. Who lived over the garage, said Miss Newcomb. Mrs. Briggs hung up so fast Miss Newcomb just waited for her. Miss Newcomb was still sitting there, because the vestibule was dark and seemed pleasant when the telephone rang again.

A Mrs. Beveridge had heard that she had a room for rent. No, said Miss Newcomb, that is, not just yet. But soon? As to that, Miss Newcomb didn't know. But before she hung up she had Mrs. Beveridge's number and address and had promised to call her the moment that she knew.

Before lunch it rang twice more. During lunch a man clear from Los Angeles said he would come out to look at the house. Miss Newcomb locked the door and drew the front blinds.

When it rang again, she didn't answer it: She was lying on her bed, and for the first time since her erysipelas her shades were drawn, though her room was on the dark side of the house. Her phone rang twice again before supper time. When she got up to get something to eat there was a car parked in the driveway and a man leaning out of the window to look at the garage. A woman got out and walked the length of the driveway to look at the door. She rang the bell, but of course Agee Ward wasn't there.

After supper the phone rang again, and this time she answered. It was long distance—a man at Mr. Kaiser's new steel plant had heard she had a room to rent. He didn't need it himself, he was paid just to find rooms for everybody else. He offered to pay her for letting him rent it for her. She wrote his number down on her telephone pad and said she would let him know. She had her coffee sitting in the dark in the room that held the evening light the longest, then, rather than turn on any lights, she went to bed. She couldn't sleep for thinking of things—then when she did sleep the phone woke her up. She got up and did three full squares in a Christmas afghan. She never had kept a clock in her room so she never knew when she got to sleep—or that the neighbor's boy sat up and read as late as he did. Some time after his light went out the fog came in. A mockingbird made such a clatter that she got up to close the window, but for some silly reason she didn't—she just stood there. She stood there until her night-gown soaked cool and damp with the fog. Then she no sooner got in bed than she was asleep.

2

When the doorbell rang Miss Newcomb was just lying in bed, not knowing whether she should get up or not. It was still foggy and she wasn't sure about her kimono; she wasn't sure whether it was still in mothballs or not. The front doorbell stopped ringing but no sooner did she lie back than she heard Mr. Ward's buzzer as well. She went to the window and peered below. A lady with a fox fur and a small round hat was peeking through the window in Mr. Ward's door. Her hat was no more than a basket with two brass pins and a piece of elastic to keep it on her hair.

Very clearly Miss Newcomb said, "Mr. Ward has been called away."

The lady with the fox fur turned and looked at her.

"I'm Mrs. Beveridge," she said, "an old school chum of Evelina, and I thought I would save you all the trouble of phoning me."

"Hmmm—" said Miss Newcomb.

"Is this the nice little house?" said Mrs. Beveridge. "Is this the nice little place for rent?"

Miss Newcomb didn't know what to say. She looked at the avocado tree, reminding herself that she must pick them, then she looked back at Mrs. Beveridge's hat.

"So far as I know," she said, "it's still Mr. Ward's place. The rent is paid up and that's as far as I know."

"Mrs. Briggs—" began Mrs. Beveridge.

"That's as far as I know," said Miss Newcomb.

"Times like these," said Mrs. Beveridge, "people might be careful when they start rumors about having a house to rent."

Miss Newcomb pushed the window down. She stood there in her bare feet while Mrs. Beveridge raced her motor and made the tires screech when she drove away. Miss Newcomb thought she might as well get right back in bed. But as she raised the window, standing at the gate at the back of the yard she saw Mrs. Frost with a fat woman and three children. Mrs. Frost was pointing down the path at Miss Newcomb's house, at the side door to the dining room. After a moment the fat lady moved. As they came down the path the little girls ran around picking the flowers and the little boy filled his pockets from the avocado tree. Miss Newcomb at first was not at home. As the little girls gathered bouquets, the little boy shifted to grapefruit, whereupon Miss Newcomb raised the window and screamed. She had not done anything like that since Chagrin Falls. The little boy ran from the yard and stood in the gate staring at her, and the little girls stood like paper dolls holding the bouquets. From the driveway the fat lady called her name. Her name was Mrs. O'Rourke and she would be pleased to look at the house Miss Newcomb had to rent.

Never before in her life had Miss Newcomb laughed in a person's face. Not even in Chagrin Falls—not in a person's face like that—and then again when Mrs. O'Rourke tripped on the sprinkler getting away. In her flight Mrs. O'Rourke went out the front, leaving her children in the back yard, and they called to each other over the roof of the house. Mrs. Bassett, Judge Ely and Mrs. Pomeroy came to see. Miss Newcomb got back in bed, and when she uncovered her head to listen she could still hear Mrs. Pomeroy and Mrs. Bassett. But in between she heard Cuchulain, so she got up.

It was like Mr. Ward to call a cat by something you couldn't call him and when you saw it written down it didn't look that way. Since Mr. Ward was gone, Cuchulain would come down and eat his meals with her, but he wouldn't sleep anywhere but at the head of the stairs. She would rather he moved in with her, since it was nights she really got lonesome, but she knew a cat's way was to get attached to a place. People could come and go so long as they didn't move the place. When she let him in she wondered who else there was she would rather see. Nobody. Now that Mrs. Ormsby had gone she would rather find Cuchulain at the door. He was black with partly long hair, which she liked because it showed breeding, but not so long that it bothered the cat in him. When he was four months old he had the flu, and when he came back from the doctor to die, it was clear to anybody who knew him that he had changed. He didn't die after all, but he did stay changed. For one thing he lost his purr—and no matter how you scratched him the most you could get was a sound as if he had a bad cold in his head. Miss Newcomb couldn't help but think he had lost his speech. When it was clear he had lost his purr she spent more time trying to understand him, as she did with people who couldn't talk very well. She decided that he said everything with his tail. By watching his tail she knew even more than when he was purring and she had reason to believe he said some things just for her. Now, when she opened the door, he was gone. She unhooked the screen to call him when suddenly he reappeared, a bird in his mouth, and the bell at his throat jingling. She slammed the screen just in time and stood listening to him. The poor thing was still alive from the way Cuchulain was growling and every now and then rattling his bell. That fool bell that she had paid 69¢ for. From the icebox she took an egg and cracked it into a saucer, then dropped the shell into last night's coffee grounds. She added a cup of water and set it on the stove. As she stood there, waiting, she could see through two rooms and the front room window, on to the corner where Mrs. O'Rourke stood. Her girls still held their bouquets but the boy was picking the bark off Judge Ely's prize cork tree. Miss Newcomb had never thought before of renting her house to anybody, and she certainly wouldn't think of renting it to Mrs. O'Rourke. But if someone like Miss Newcomb with a husband to keep up the yard—if someone like that came along, well, why shouldn't she? She could move into Mr. Ward's rooms until he came home. She and Cuchulain, who lived up there anyhow. Think of all the fuss and bother it would save not having to move all of his things—for he was only missing— he might turn up any time. She remembered the actual case of a man who was missing for seven years, then turned up just as spry as when he went away. She wouldn't promise to keep Mr! Ward's things that long, but that was something to think about anyhow. When the phone rang she was thinking about it and when Mrs. Briggs asked about Mr. Ward's rooms she said she just might move up there. It would keep it for him and be less work for her. A seven-room house and a garden was just too much for her. So if Mrs. Briggs happened to know a nice quiet couple without any children——

Mrs. Briggs broke in to ask how much.

Miss Newcomb hadn't thought of that, she hadn't thought of that at all, but she remembered that Mrs. Pomeroy was paying fifty-five. Fifty-five for five rooms and one bath.

"For seven rooms and two baths—shower upstairs and tub down—I think sixty-five," Miss Newcomb said.

Somebody who was not Mrs. Briggs answered her. She wanted to know where it was there was a seven-room house for sixty-five dollars—or for that matter for seventy-five dollars if that would help.

[150]

Miss Newcomb had forgotten she was on a party line. Up till last night she used the phone so little she didn't really need one at all—except for being her age and all alone in the house. Now Evelina Briggs and the woman were fighting and there was nothing she could say so she put the receiver down and stood up. Right away it started ringing again but she could smell her coffee burning and had to run and look at it. She put on a pan for her egg and as it fried she felt a little giddy—or what she felt that giddy people must feel. She felt like flipping the egg or doing something like that. With the pancake turner she scraped the egg loose from the pan and was considering the flip motion when her doorbell rang. But before she could leave the kitchen she heard the voice of Evelina Briggs. "Don't bother," Evelina called. "I'll just let myself in!" And when Miss Newcomb entered the room, there she was.

Evelina Briggs had once had an eight-week part in a drama that during the ninth week went to New York. This had permanently altered her voice. Miss Newcomb could not help but think of Cuchulain and his lost purr—though Evelina had certainly not lost anything. Quite the contrary, yet Miss Newcomb always thought of him. Something had happened to both of them so that they lost their normal speech and what you heard now was a makeshift of some kind. Evelina was a full—as she said herself—a full armful of woman, with a tendency to get out of hand. But Miss Newcomb had never remarked before just what happened when she sat down, for there she was, and without any lap at all. Her lap folded up and sat beside her, like baby twins. Ever since she could remember, Miss Newcomb had heard—as alone as she was she still couldn't help hearing—that Evelina Briggs had a way with the men. It was puzzling to wonder what it could be. Miss Newcomb's way with men had stopped with the young man who liked to stand, wherever he stood, with his fingers just touching her hips. She had never got over the feeling that something was following her.

"Well, dearie," said Evelina, holding out a check, "I decided that your rent is eighty a month. If you're going to have a ceiling you might as well get started with a good one——"

"Who?" said Miss Newcomb.

"Spavic," said Evelina. "The name is Spavic. I'll have to admit that the name isn't so hot but the boy went here to college—says he knew Agee Ward. Nice quiet boy—says he knows you too."

"Me?" said Miss Newcomb.

"And he's a poet," said Evelina, "like Mr. Ward."

"Mr. Ward," said Miss Newcomb, "is an *artist*—not a poet."

"You mean to tell me," said Evelina, "that you haven't read his poems? That he lived here and didn't leave you his poems?"

"He didn't live *here!*" said Miss Newcomb. "He lived over the garage, and whatever he left is still up in his rooms. What he did in his rooms was his own private business, and if that's what he did, why he's free to do it. There's people who read, so I suppose there's people who write."

"I wasn't complaining—" said Evelina.

"It's a free country," said Miss Newcomb. "I'd rather a boy did something useful but I suppose this country is free. He's gone and lost himself just to keep it that way."

To change the subject Evelina said, "You ever live in Chicago?"

"Chagrin Falls," said Miss Newcomb, "until nineteen twenty-three, and then"—she patted her lap with her hand—"right *here*."

"Well," said Evelina, "that's where they're from. It's quite a town—it's quite a dump." As she got up to leave, her skirt circled her hips in heavy folds that explained where her lap had gone. She smoothed it flat and stood patting her tummy bulge. "How's it," she said, "in the rear, dearie?"

"Very nice," said Miss Newcomb. "Very, very nice."

"You're telling me!" said Evelina Briggs, and then she was gone.

3

MISSING MAN NAMES

LOCAL LADY

NEAREST KIN

When she opened the door for Cuchulain Miss Newcomb bent over to pick up the paper, then she remained there as if she had a crick in her back. She read it through once in that position, then she straightened up to look at the picture as there were bubble spots rising before her eyes. If it hadn't been for the arrow she wouldn't even have known him—and what a sight he was behind that Darcy Munger with his big eyes! Standing in the vestibule, she read again that Agee Ward, promising local artist, had named Miss Augusta Newcomb,

his landlady, as nearest of kin. It went on to say how widely
Mr. Ward had traveled and how his paintings were in the
country's leading museums. Many people would remember Mr.
Ward, it said, as the author of a volume of poems and for
his colorful murals in the wing of the library. Miss Newcomb,
it said in closing, had removed here twenty years ago from
Chagrin Falls.

In the kitchen Miss Newcomb cleaned the pot and put on
fresh coffee although she had already had her morning cup.
Before sitting down to think about it she went to the door and
called Cuchulain, bringing him along to sit in her lap while
she read it again. Miss Newcomb never read anything but the
papers and sometimes she thought that was a waste, but now
she wondered what that boy had been up to. Very likely there
was some relation between what he did and the windows
being covered, but for someone who moved out here for the
sunshine it was hard to understand. What he did in his room
was his own business, except that she had spoken to him—
no, she had written him a note saying that he could do as
he pleased but not to *paint* up there. Whenever she thought
of him painting she saw the floor of the college art class, a
floor so spattered you would think a thousand pigeons were
living in there. But he did all of his painting in a barn somewhere else. Every morning he would leave—and now she remembered the colored glasses he always wore. He never left
the house without them, or if he did he went back in. It was
Judge Ely himself who stopped Mr. Ward right in front of
his house to ask in a very loud voice what it was that was
wrong with him. Judge Ely's father had been a physician and
he took a great interest in strange diseases, and would always

[154]

stop anyone that looked a little that way. As a matter of fact, Mr. Ward didn't look just right. Whether it was the way he walked around or his glasses, for a man as young as he was he didn't look normal; he didn't step out and go places like young men do. But that had been his own business and she never questioned him. That day Judge Ely had stopped him and in such a loud voice asked if he was sick—that day she had listened because Judge Ely was so deaf. If Mr. Ward was going to answer she might as well hear it too. But all he had done was slap Judge Ely on the shoulder just a little hard for such an old man, and then stand there laughing at him. She still thought that a very rude thing to do. But it got Judge Ely to laughing and soon they were both laughing so hard Judge Ely had to lean on Mr. Ward. It was one of the funniest things she had even seen. Judge Ely got to laughing so hard he let himself right down on the lawn and though his mouth was open, not a sound came out. For a while she had been certain that he would die laughing. Mr. Ward had just left for a walk but he had to come back and lean on the house, and ten minutes later she could still hear him laughing up-stairs. She would swear on a Bible he hadn't said a thing. All he did was start laughing and somehow get the old man to laughing, leaving him there on the lawn like he had gone silly. But after that neither of them said anything. Up till then Judge Ely often asked him to play croquet, but after that he never asked him again. They would nod but they never said anything. Sometimes she thought it was because they were ashamed they had been so silly—other times she didn't know what she thought. One sure thing was that her own laughing had changed. Even when she had laughed at that woman—

as hard as she had laughed in years—she had the feeling that something else was happening to her. That's all—just that something else was happening to her.

When Cuchulain wanted down she put him out. She gathered up her broom, her cedar mop, and a dust cloth, and on her way down the drive scooped up Cuchulain again. He was pestering the birds in Mrs. Pomeroy's window-box and she scolded him. To put an end to that she carried him with her to the top of the stairs. When she put him down he wanted in and stood there making a great racket, meowing and rubbing against the door. It was a fine thing to stand and watch, and made her sick again to think what some people thought of cats.

As she opened the door Cuchulain ran in and skidded on the turn he made for the kitchen. There was his saucer with a deep green mold growing in it. Right up till then she hadn't felt a thing, she hadn't put her mind on what it is to be *missing,* but when she saw the saucer she had to turn and sit down on something. There was nothing to sit on but two low things that she nearly fell getting into, a chair, or whatever it was, no more than eight inches off the floor. But once there it wasn't bad, and she closed her eyes. It was even rather nice having the windows covered, and if she felt like that very often, or was subject to fainting, she might *do* a room that way herself. When she opened her eyes she saw a very bad stain on the ceiling, kidney shaped, and she made a note to have that leak repaired. And then she heard the wildest kind of noise in the tub. She pushed herself up and from the door to the bathroom saw Cuchulain chasing his tail, around and around, banking himself sharply on the walls of the tub. He had never

[156]

carried on like this while living with her. He had had free access to her tub, to everything she had in the house, but he had never let himself carry on like this. He would eat with her —but he did his *living* up here. Now they could both eat and live together and she wondered how it was, how it had been that she never thought of this before.

As suddenly as he had started this game, Cuchulain stopped, and left the tub. He went between her legs into the front room and settled in the spot that she had just left. Its being so close to the floor didn't seem to bother him. The one thing she would like to ask Agee Ward—and she would ask him the next time she saw him—was why a grown-up person should sit so close to the floor. It was just that much farther up and that much farther down. She would bring up a chair she could sit in without risking her life to get to it, and one she could get out of without pushing on her knees. Otherwise she would leave it pretty much as it was. She didn't like so many books around, but at least it was something different—and that was the only reason she went to Ocean Park every spring. Wondering which of her chairs to bring up, she turned to have a look at the bedroom—a part of the front room behind curtains with a hunting scene. As she drew aside the curtains she said, "*Oh, heavenly Peter!*"

She hadn't said that for years—not since the ladies' choir in Chagrin Falls when she had to say something the Sunday her petticoat fell all the way down. She had to leave it in a puddle at her feet and come back later for it. Now she said, "*Oh, heavenly Peter!*" again as she looked at the business on the floor. She had forgotten what he'd done with the bed, that he had taken the frame downstairs, and that only the springs, the springs and the mattress, remained upstairs. And there they were—right down on the floor. She didn't even want to stoop that far. How he ever made it she couldn't imagine—though from the look of it, it hadn't been made for some time. Just the monk's cloth spread thrown back and a very smooth hollow between the pillows. As she wondered about this, Cuchulain strolled in and filled it up.

He was certainly right at home—and she might feel at home herself when she got the bed up to where a person could get into it. She would do that first, and she turned to leave the room but her arm bumped something off the radiator. It was an album, left—of all places—on top of the radiator, and when it fell one of the pictures had dropped out. This was a picture of the Eiffel Tower and Miss Newcomb stood looking at it, wondering again what people ever did with such a thing. On the back she saw that it was addressed to *Peter Spavic*—and this was the reason she glanced to see what the message was. For it did seem strange that a card belonging to Peter Spavic should fall out of an album belonging to Agee Ward. Holding the card to the light, she read:

The only obscene women . . .

but at the word *obscene* the card slipped from her hand. It dropped on her left foot, which kicked at it as if it were a bug, and before she could stop doing that the card was under the spring. There she left it and started across the room. At the door she remembered Cuchulain, but while she was saying *kitty-kitty* she could hear a voice speaking to her. She could swear it was right there in the room and over and over it kept saying, *Before it's too late, Miss Newcomb, you go downstairs.* Just for that reason she didn't leave the room. Just for that reason she once sat with a man all the way from Omaha to Denver, although the voice told her to sit in the ladies' room. Now, with her own voice, she asked Cuchulain what he would like to eat, and she came back in and turned the refrigerator on.

4

Miss Newcomb was standing in the door of the garage wondering just where Agee Ward might have put the bed ends, when she heard someone coming up behind her. He kept clearing his throat all the way but waited to spit till he was right beside her, and she heard it rattle the bushes along the drive.

"Ma'am," he said, "you this Miss Newcomb?"

Miss Newcomb turned and looked at him. He was a very big man and she knew him as well as she knew anybody—not very well, that is, but enough to talk to in the street. He raised oranges and things and always wore the same dirty pants and the kind of hat the men in the first war used to wear. She had never seen him without his pipe, but now he took it out, fooled with it, then put it back in his mouth so he could talk.

"I'd no idea you was Miss Newcomb," he said. She didn't know just how to take that and he said, "I used to speak with Mr. Ward often. I kept wonderin' to myself what had become of him."

"He's missing," she said.

"That's what I just read in the *Advance*." He took the paper out of his rear pocket and unrolled it. To find the place he had to put his glasses on and turn his back to her to get the light on it. "Missing man names local woman nearest kin," he read. "I had no idea," he said, "that boy was your kin."

Miss Newcomb was about to say she hadn't either—but she didn't, she didn't somehow. Instead she said, "Right up till now I don't think we've really been introduced." But she didn't mean it the way it sounded; she didn't want him to take off his hat and stand there patting down what little hair he had.

"Well, now," he was saying, "now can you beat that," and he looked all around in case someone could beat it. "I been around here so long," he said, "I figured the birds knew me."

They laughed at that, then Miss Newcomb said she knew him as well as her own name, only his name, somehow, was always escaping her.

"No more than I had any idea you was *Miss* Newcomb," he said.

Well, there it was, and very plain, and feeling very warm Miss Newcomb said that right up till today she wasn't sure what his name really was.

"Bloom," he said, "the flower kind, the sweet smelly kind." He laughed at that till he saw she wasn't laughing, then he spit and said, "And here you are his nearest kin."

"No," she said, "I'm not. I'm not his kin at all; I'm just his landlady."

"Then why'd he say you were?"

"I've no idea," she said, "unless it was he didn't have any

and all of his things are here." She looked over the garage at his rooms and Mr. Bloom looked too.

"I knew there was something about that boy," he said.

"What was that?" she said.

"His bein' an artist——"

"Oh——" she said, and felt very foolish though there was no reason she should.

"I knew there was something about that boy," said Mr. Bloom, "not so much from what he said but how he said it. Sometimes take a day or two for me to catch up with him."

"You knew him well?" said Miss Newcomb.

"Well, never really introduced——" said Mr. Bloom. He looked at her but she looked right straight down the drive. "Seems he used to take his walk right by my place when I was waterin' or weedin', and we nearly always got a word in about somethin'."

"He was a nice boy," she said.

"I'd have give a lot to've known him better," said Mr. Bloom. "I don't know as we saw eye to eye but at least we saw somethin'." His pipe went out and he raised the sole of his right boot to scratch a match on it. Seeing him standing there on one leg, Miss Newcomb remembered the bed ends.

"Mr. Bloom," she said, "you have a minute to spare?" Mr. Bloom said he had. "Mr. Ward," said Miss Newcomb, "liked to sleep right down near the floor—he liked to sit right down near the floor too."

"Well——" said Mr. Bloom.

"The thing is——" began Miss Newcomb, then she wished she hadn't brought the thing up at all. There was no other word she could think of for bed except *bed*. *Couch* was even worse.

Since *bed* had always been all right before, she wondered why it wasn't all right now. She looked at Mr. Bloom who had his sleeves rolled up and so much hair on his arms.

"Now why d'you think he did that?" said Mr. Bloom.

"The thing is," said Miss Newcomb, "other people might not, and I wondered if you happened to have a minute to spare."

"Sure thing," said Mr. Bloom, and walked past her into the garage. When she followed him in she could smell him and she wondered how much of it was his pipe and how much of it was what a man like that smelled like.

"What you lookin' for—the bed?" he said.

"Yes," she said.

Mr. Bloom walked right over to it. It made her think that he must have seen it even before he asked her that.

"Now where you want it?" he said.

"Up—" she said, and hurried to get in front of him. "Up," she repeated, "upstairs."

"Here I come," he said, and she ran right up the stairs ahead of him.

"Just like a spring chicken," she heard him say, not so much to someone as just to himself, "a sprrringg chicken," he repeated, and then he was on his way up.

Until Mr. Bloom came in she had no idea how small the room was. It was just impossible for him to come in and help put the bed up at the same time, so they had to stop and think about it. While she thought about it Mr. Bloom kept repeating, "I knew it, I knew it all the time." Until she had to ask him what, although she knew what he was going to say.

"I knew that boy read or somethin'," he said.

The moment he put down the bed Mr. Bloom took off his hat and Miss Newcomb knew it wasn't just for her; in fact, it wasn't for her at all so much as it was for the room. She had never thought of people who read in that light; in fact, she had simply never thought of them except as people who had never had anything useful to do. And here was Mr. Bloom flushed in the face and half beside himself. He went over to where he could read the titles but first put his hands behind him, as if out of the way, and his legs backed off with him as if his pants might touch. His mouth was open and he had let his pipe go out.

"You like to read?" said Miss Newcomb.

"No, ma'am," he said, "I don't." When she didn't answer that he said, "But I sure respect people who do!"

Miss Newcomb thought that about the strangest point of view she had ever heard.

"I suppose," said Mr. Bloom, "you don't do nothin' else."

"I don't read at all," she said, but Mr. Bloom hadn't even been listening.

"Do you suppose," he said, "Mr. Ward read all of the books he's got here?"

"If he didn't," she said, "I don't know why he bought them since there isn't much else you can do with books." Mr. Bloom hadn't heard that either—he was still bent over, his lips reading the titles and his face like a man saying his prayers.

In a voice of decision Miss Newcomb said, "Mr. Bloom, I want to thank you very much——"

"But we ain't put it up yet," said Mr. Bloom, and put on his hat. So he could get in the bedroom Miss Newcomb backed out and Mr. Bloom tipped up the spring, right on end, and started to fasten on the ends. Miss Newcomb was so stunned by the sight on the floor she just stood there staring at it—fearing either to call Mr. Bloom's attention to it or to let it pass. Wads of sweepings had gathered in rolls, some of them like storm clouds with bits of white in them, and in between on the floor was every manner of thing. Buttons, cigarettes used and unused, one blue, one brown and one red sock, a ping-pong ball, a piece of chewed fat, a tube of hair oil that had leaked a stain, several pencils, and a small brass Chinese cat. But worst of all, there was that postcard she had dropped. It was right side up, the writing so clear she thought she could read it from where she stood, and while Mr. Bloom held up the bed she reached for it.

"That cat," she said in a loud voice, "that cat!"

Without so much as looking Mr. Bloom said, "Cat of mine just littered—you know someone wants a cat?"

"No," she said, and left the room to put the postcard somewhere. Mr. Ward's album was stuck in with his books—where she had finally decided to put it—and now she slipped the postcard between some of the leaves.

"There's that one," said Mr. Bloom, and waded through the dirt to the other end. A green marble rolled out from one cloud of dust slowly across the floor. Miss Newcomb was half bent over for it when Cuchulain came in from the hall and hit it right between her legs under the bed again. Then he was right in the center of it, snooping and scratching around.

"Kitty-kitty," said Mr. Bloom, "kitty-kitty."

Miss Newcomb hadn't thought about it at all, but when she heard him say that, standing there in all that dirt, she knew what he was. He was a bachelor—no married man would ever act like that.

Then he said, "Lady—while I'm holdin' this up, why don't you get your mop and wipe under here."

She should of thought of that so she said, "Mr. Bloom, a lady first sweeps it."

"Well, sweep it then!" he said, in a way that hurried her for a broom. She was right back in and swept it out, even around his shoes.

"It's like blowin' your nose," he said.

Miss Newcomb looked up at him, not understanding.

"Where's it all come from?" he said. "In your head, under the bed, where's it all come from?"

Miss Newcomb left the rest as it was and hurried the pan downstairs. She went out in back to the incinerator and burned it up. She was still there when Mr. Bloom came back with all of the pencils he had found when he let the bed down again. They had been right in it somewhere, he said. She had nothing to say to that but thanked him very coolly for his help, and he said it was worth it just to get a look at Mr. Ward's room. Just to get a look at books like that, he said.

She reminded him there were doubtless more books in the library.

"But these were *read* books," he said; "these were books he read."

To that she didn't have anything to say. On his way out he picked some of her grass to run through the stem of his pipe and then a leaf to chew from her avocado tree. She stayed at the incinerator until every little bit had burned.

5

With her tea Miss Newcomb stood at the window and remembered the time she had spoken to Agee Ward for his own good. He had come out of the house with one brown sock and one blue one. For his own good she stopped him and said, "So brown and blue are your favorite colors?" And he had stopped right there in the driveway and laughed at them. Then he had said, "Miss Newcomb, do you like maple sugar?" "I like maple sugar very much," she had said. Then he went right back upstairs and came down with some. He did all of that without changing his socks at all. There they were, still brown and blue, and she couldn't help notice that the blue one was dirty—perhaps the mate to the one she had just found under the bed.

One evening she had been standing at the window when that opossum that ate her grapes, on his way up the vine, stopped and peered in at her. They had both been so shocked that they hadn't moved. She had stood there pouring hot coffee all over the front of her dress but he didn't leave until she burned herself and dropped everything. Then he didn't leave—he just went on up the vine. She had not been more than ten inches away from his long nose, staring at her, but she couldn't tell you what an opossum really looked like at all. There was something like that about herself and Mr. Ward. Not that he looked like an opossum—far from it, he was sometimes a nice-looking boy—but for the life of her she couldn't tell you *how* he looked. It was always such a surprise, a real surprise, even when she stood waiting for him, that like the opossum she never noticed his looks.

But however it is you know about people she could see that she knew about him pretty well, without ever coming to a showdown, that is. Somehow she had known all along that he was the kind of person who just *might* say what she had read upstairs. And if he had ever said that—why, then where would she have been? Or where would Mr. Bloom be for that matter, hearing something like that? She had known all along that the way to protect herself was to say something and while he was answering walk away laughing at it. Say anything, but be sure and laugh at it. Yet it was a very strange thing—now that she thought about it—that she had laughed and laughed without really knowing why. For a year she had laughed with him at something, sometimes she had stood in the door, still laughing, and seen Mrs. Pomeroy wondering what it was they were laughing at. Sometimes she had laughed longer and harder just because Mrs. Pomeroy was there. And that was a mad thing to have done since she hadn't known any more than Mrs. Pomeroy what in the world it was that she was laughing at. Or why, when she stopped, she felt so good.

6

The first things Miss Newcomb found in Mr. Ward's closet were three pajama tops hanging on a nail—but not a bottom, not a single bottom anywhere. The conclusion to be drawn from this, that Mr. Ward slept all winter without them, she decided to put off until she had had her lunch. The tops themselves were progressively soiled, beginning with very dirty, plain dirty, and nearly clean—and the nearly clean tops he sometimes wore when he went out for the mail. Whether he kept them for this purpose was something else to think about.

From her kitchen Miss Newcomb brought up some things and made her lunch in Mr. Ward's front room. Lettuce, liverwurst, whole-wheat bread, and cottage cheese. She sat at the window overlooking Mrs. Pomeroy's yard and the clothes she had drying in the sun. One of Mrs. Pomeroy's bushes grew right up to the edge of the window and the bees were noisy in the blossoms. It was just like being on a picnic or something. When she had backed up to sit down in Mr. Ward's funny chair her skirt had caught on one corner of it. And that was something that happened on a picnic too. And eating down so low this way, her knees sticking up where she could lean on them, was just what she did on most picnics. Right across from her was her own real chair and one she didn't have to fall into, but if she sat there she had to look at the wall. And on that wall was a picture that bothered her.

There was a small town square with a fountain in the middle and a road going out of it on the other side. But on both sides of the square were the very same buildings, with the same names and even the same barber pole. The only difference she could see was that on one side it seemed to be morning, and that on the other side it was evening, and getting dark. The street itself went on out of town, but right at the edge of town it got fuzzy as if there was nothing out there that he could paint. And that was about all there was to it. On one side of the street it was morning, and sun so bright it made her blink—and on the other side it was evening and in the shade. And to make it worse there were the oddest street lights she'd ever seen. They were burning on both sides of the street but not really making any light—they were like fireflies or the radium numbers on a watch. In the street there was nobody anywhere and it was a kind of spooky picture even though it didn't mean anything. It was in a gold frame with a metal plate that said JOURNEY'S END.

Because of this she sat in the low chair and looked at a picture called JOURNEY OUT. It was an old house like she had seen in Chagrin Falls. It was just like a man to paint what hadn't been painted itself, and probably think that he had taken care of it. It was a fine big house with two floors and a very fine attic, and on the first floor was a porch half the way around. When she was a girl in Chagrin Falls important people lived in such houses, but even before she left those people had moved out. They used them for funeral parlors now, or something like that. When she was a girl one man's family was enough for one of those houses, but today four or five families would be living there. There were such houses in the city, and with her own eyes she had sometimes seen as many as a dozen mailboxes out in front. It was a mighty good thing those old people died. That important people died just the same as anyone else. It would kill people like that to know that instead of painting the house there were people who sat out in front and drew pictures of it. When she was a girl a lady like her would have been an aunt to somebody and still be living behind one of those windows in the top. Coming down in the morning for breakfast, sometimes for tea—and in February to see who the new babies were. There would be some uncles around and at least a grandfather or two. And now there it was—a funeral parlor or something. What had happened to the country had been the same as that. Nobody had asked her

—but she would have said it all started when they left Grandpa instead of waiting for Grandpa to leave them. They left the aunts and uncles, then they started leaving themselves, even leaving the children—if there were children to leave. That was the way they settled it. They could do as they wanted because there was nothing left to leave.

She must have fallen asleep looking at the house. It was nearly two, and time for her nap, but she made it a point never to nap in her chair. It was a rule, besides being uncomfortable. Strange as it was, there was something restful about Mr. Ward's chair. Her hands slipped into her lap where Cuchulain, until then, had been sound asleep. Now he moved to the top of the table where he finished off her cottage cheese.

A prolonged ringing of the doorbell woke her up. Until she was up on her feet she thought it was another dream she was having. She stopped at the sink to wet her eyes, then went to the head of the stairs and bent down low to see who it was. An elderly couple and a young man. As she went down the stairs she knew she had seen the young man before, right here in fact, right here in the yard. He was the boy that sometimes did things for Agee Ward. Mr. Ward had said that he was free to come and go—or come up without ringing as he nearly always did.

"Miss Newcomb," he said, "I suppose you remember me?"

"Why—yes," she said.

"I'm Peter Spavic," he said, "and my father and mother would like to rent your house."

Mr. and Mrs. Spavic smiled at her. Mr. Spavic was very

lean and twice opened his mouth as if to speak, but neither time did he say anything. Instead he put his hand on the back of his head and rubbed the short hair.

"I'm awfully sorry," said Miss Newcomb, "but Mrs. Briggs of the *Advance*——"

"She sent us up," said Peter Spavic.

"Oh!" said Miss Newcomb. "Oh, of course. I knew perfectly well but all this moving——" She stopped when Mr. Spavic, for the third time, opened his mouth and raised his finger. For the third time he didn't say anything.

"My mother and father," Peter said, "knew Mr. Ward in Chicago."

"Yah!" Mr. Spavic said, as if someone had clapped him on the back. It came out of him with such force that Miss Newcomb stepped back a ways. Mr. Spavic looked at each one of them, then folded his arms.

Miss Newcomb opened the screen and came outside. Peter Spavic was watching her so she said, "And you knew Mr. Ward in Chicago?"

"Oh, yes!" Peter said, and started to laugh. It was a very personal laugh, in short jets and a little raucous, and Miss Newcomb knew that the joke was not for her. It was not a joke for anybody except Peter Spavic and he walked away by himself to enjoy it. It was a very queer thing to do but Mrs. Spavic herself was so upset that Miss Newcomb did what she could to ignore it.

"The house is in such a mess," she said, turning and smiling at Mrs. Spavic. "If you people had just let me know—had called——"

"OHHHHHHHhhhhhhhhh—" said Mrs. Spavic, and Miss

Newcomb saw that Mrs. Spavic was all right. There was nothing in her face that she could really stop and look at, just a tired red face, but she liked it anyhow. Mr. Spavic unfolded his arms and walked ahead to hold the screen open while she and Mrs. Spavic walked in. Peter remained where he was near the garage. He stood looking off at whatever he had seen and the sight of it still tickled him.

Miss Newcomb began by showing Mrs. Spavic the downstairs and the spot to watch during the winter rains. Then they went upstairs and looked awhile at that. Whenever Mr. Spavic looked at a corner or any place that things came together, his mouth would open and he would lean back. But nothing came out until he saw something on the stairs. Right when she was showing Mrs. Spavic the laundry chute to the basement Mr. Spavic made another one of those sounds. Then right after it came the words, "You build thees 'ouse?" He made these sounds wide apart, and though she hadn't seen his face Miss Newcomb thought she could see his mouth shaping them. Making motions like people saying vowels. When she turned and said no, she had just bought it, Mr. Spavic looked so happy his eyes swelled.

Looking at him Mrs. Spavic said, "It's no worry—he bills 'ouses." And shook her head at what a silly habit he had.

"So lonk," said Mr. Spavic, "you not built it."

"Oh no—oh my, no," Miss Newcomb said. She looked at the spot Mr. Spavic looked at, wondering what it was that was wrong, and Mr. Spavic made motions with his hands. With one hand he made a spreading motion; the other slowly worked itself around something he saw in the air.

Mrs. Spavic said, "Gregor is good insite, outsite 'ouses."

[172]

"The truth is," said Miss Newcomb, "it's just more than I can do, all alone and with a garden in the back."

"Gregor is not bat growink," Mrs. Spavic said. They both turned and looked at Gregor who was tapping the wall with his finger as a doctor sounds a patient's chest. His eyes were lidded and he was making a ssshhhh-ssshhhhing sound—then he found what he was after, rapped on it.

"A perry pox," he said.

"He means a perry pox," said Mrs. Spavic, and shaped one with her hands. "Gooseperry—strawperry—plueperry pox."

"Well, now—" said Miss Newcomb, and shook her head.

"An yet," said Mrs. Spavic, "if you like us, we like it."

"A perry pox," Gregor repeated.

"I think you're just the people," said Miss Newcomb. "I've wanted somebody so bad in the garden and——"

"He surprise you," said Mrs. Spavic. "Gregor, he surprise efryone."

Miss Newcomb had a feeling Mrs. Spavic was right. At the foot of the stairs Gregor was peeling a board loose with his thumb; a splayed blue-black thumbnail pried it up easily.

"I feex it," he said, and went off somewhere. When they reached the front door he was on his way back with a tool box, and while they stood there talking he fixed it. He left the tool box under the sink in the kitchen and then joined them.

"Where is Peter?" he said.

They looked up and down the driveway but Peter was not there.

"Pee-ter!" Mrs. Spavic called, and using the palm of his hands like a paddle Mr. Spavic made a sound that made their ears ring. From Mr. Ward's rooms over the garage Peter answered. Miss Newcomb was so shocked she simply couldn't say anything. She waited for Mr. Spavic to act, but when he didn't she went down the driveway and up the stairs two steps at a time. Peter Spavic was sitting in her chair reading a book. He had pushed her lunch to one side so he could put his feet on the table and Cuchulain was sprawled asleep in his lap.

"Young man," she said, then wondered what she should say. Peter Spavic stopped blowing his nose, and looked at her. "Mr. Ward," she said, "Mr. Ward is missing—and while he——"

"Missing?" he said. *"Him* missing?"

Miss Newcomb had to say something so she said, "It was in the paper—on the front page of the paper."

"I don't read it," he said. He put the book back in its place on the shelf and came to the door. "Is he—" he said, "is he really—*missing?*"

"Mr. Ward is reported missing," she said. While he looked at her she could see the blood leave his face. He was a very blond boy and without the blood his face looked jaundiced and his sandy sun-faded hair brittle as dry grass. For a moment Miss Newcomb thought she would have to help hold him up. Then right at the foot of the stairs Mrs. Spavic called, "Pe-ter," and he walked stiffly into the hall. He went downstairs and walked past Mrs. Spavic at the door. When Miss Newcomb got outside he was nowhere to be seen but Mr. and Mrs. Spavic were waiting for her.

"If it's no worry," Mrs. Spavic said, "Tuesday, Wednesday—sometime, anytime?"

"Any time," Miss Newcomb said, "just any time."

Then she walked with them toward the front, naming the flowers for Mrs. Spavic, until they came to Peter Spavic sitting on the curb. He was chewing on the long-stemmed grass that grew like sprinkler leaks in the yard. He neither looked up nor looked at her, and when Mr. and Mrs. Spavic walked away he got up and followed them down the street. He walked just far enough behind so that Mrs. Spavic was always a little troubled, and kept turning her head to see if he was there. But at the corner he sprinted up front and was soon so far ahead that Mrs. Spavic was calling, "Pee-ter, Peeee-ter!"

Her own chair she put off until Mr. Spavic could help her, but everything else Miss Newcomb brought up by herself. There wasn't much—there simply wasn't room. Food from her icebox, a few pots and pans, summer dresses and house shoes. Other things could be added as she remembered them. There being nothing but books upstairs she decided to move only one of her own, *The Complete Gardener,* with 983 illustrations. The leather-bound *Beacon Lights of History* she left in the wall shelf. The Spavics didn't impress her as very literary people and might not have any books of their own to put in there. When she had sent the measurements to a bookstore in the city they had sent her the *Beacon Lights of History* as a perfect fit. And so they were—what they had sent to her. Not until four years later did Miss Newcomb discover that volume thirteen was not in the set. She had written them about it and they sent her one in a different binding which she kept on the side table for a year. In just one year the color faded till she could hardly read the title and she had to keep *The Complete Gardener* on it to keep it flat. So this spring she had given it away. A truck had come around asking for books for "Our Boys," and she had given it to them.

If it ever came around again she would hardly know what to do. She doubted very much if even a person like Mr. Ward had any idea how many books he had up here. But it would be just like her to give away one he knew about. She could tell some that he knew about by the cards sticking up in them —and there was a card sticking up in the album too. To think that she had nearly forgotten about that! On one side she could see just the top of the Eiffel Tower, but as for the other side, well, she didn't know. Without moving—just reaching—she pulled up the card to where she could read the three words she already knew. On the line beneath were the words— but before she read them she turned away and as quiet as she could locked the door. There she was, locked in with it, but instead of just walking back to peek she walked right over and pulled it all the way out. Holding it with both hands, she turned her back to the window, and then stood waiting until it stopped jumping up and down.

> The only obscene women I know are
> in *Vogue* and *Harper's Bazaar*.
> Reflect on this.

Nobody struck her down, so she read it once more then raised her head and repeated, aloud, to the room, *Reflect on this*. It was like something she had done in Sunday school one time. Reflecting on this, she placed the card near the middle of *The Complete Gardener*, the tip showing, just as Mr. Ward would have done. Then she took a pan and went out into the garden to pick Swiss chard.

In the spring of the valley's worst flood, and with her own basement half full of water, Miss Newcomb had gone to the city because of what was called her change of life. There had really been none, none at all, but it had been nice to get out of the house and sit in an office reading *Harper's Bazaar*. It had seemed a little strange, but she wouldn't have said *that*. No. Most of the girls were a little thin but she supposed it was what they were wearing, and things like that simply weren't to be had in the larger sizes. Goodness knows where they would wear them, except to have their pictures taken or live for a while in a foreign country or on a boat. Most of them were a little thin—but let them grow up and go about living, or having a family, and there wouldn't be much of that. There were very likely other pictures she hadn't seen. Or maybe the same thing had happened to it that had happened to everything else, with these movie people standing in front of everything. Or look what had happened to Sears & Roebuck and Montgomery Ward. There was a time a stout lady could get some idea how she looked by referring to the corset section. Now the stoutest ladies were little more than plump. She could hardly remember a time she hadn't been stouter than that and would have laughed to think of putting a corset on. And on top of that they sold through the mail little padded things for flat ladies to wear—and now that she thought of it maybe *that* was what he meant. But she would have to look at *Harper's Bazaar* again to make sure. And she would like to know how it was that *he* found that out.

7

Every Saturday, following her nap, Miss Newcomb shopped at the Market Basket. Since there were no more deliveries, she had to bring everything home herself in a contraption that cost her two dollars and thirty-five cents. It was periwinkle blue, according to the lady that sold it to her, and had VICTORY SHOPPER'S SPECIAL painted on in gold. Because of the little wooden wheels that might break going over curbings, she had got so she always walked a certain way. Three drive-ins east of her own she would cross the street to where Mrs. Bagley's pottery goose stood in the yard. Mrs. Haupt had brought it to her all the way from Bavaria, and it was so life-like that strangers would stop and say whatever it is you say when you want to call a goose. After three years Miss Newcomb was still deceived by it. At night Mrs. Bagley took it in since the time some young vandals cracked eggs under it and left a dozen little chicks loose in the yard. For a year even the smartest birds were fooled—but now even the dumb ones had learned better and just out of meanness did what only birds can do.

In the sun on Primavera was the Bowling Green where the men rolled bowls across the lawn, and if they were there Miss Newcomb always looked at them. That meant that she had to walk in the sun clear to the corner, but there was something about it that she liked. She liked the smoothness of the grass, cut so short it was like a table, and the men standing together the funny way men stand. If she walked slow she could see the bowl make a long arc toward something, and maybe come to a slow stop right beside it. If it did the old men would snap their fingers and relight their pipes. It was a very dull game from what she could tell about it, but there was the grass and the sound of the balls like sheep cropping. Maybe it was living out here that had made her so awfully fond of grass—sometimes all she wanted to do was sit and look at it. As she sometimes did on hot days, watching the bowling. There were benches in the park from which she could see the bowls curve and read the sign on the door of the clubroom. She could not explain why it was the sign fascinated her. It had only been hung there—she could see the string it was on through the window—but in ten years nobody had taken it down.

LAWN BOWLING

A Way of Bringing Life
into the Community
Without Marring Its Beauty

It was there today and Miss Newcomb read it again. There was something about what it said that she didn't fully understand, like there was about *Vogue* and *Harper's Bazaar*—or that saying, *"The king is dead—long live the king!"* For the life of her she couldn't make sense out of that. And yet she had the feeling that sense was there—or something more than sense—so she couldn't stop wondering about it. They were saying more than they said—both of them.

Thinking of this, she stopped at the five-way corner of Princeton and Buena Vista, and looked carefully at four of them. The onions growing in the yard of Mrs. Gage's Nursing Home were already too big for anything. Of all the things to plant for a house full of people living together—and then, after all that work, letting them go to seed. There was just no sense to it, and she crossed the street catty-cornered rather than have to look at it all close up.

But in spite of that Victor had spotted her. Not with his eyes, heaven knows; with his face squashed in that way, and living with all those onions it could hardly be his nose. It was just some special sense he had. Victor was Mrs. Bagley's dog, but either because he didn't like ducks—or thought a.wooden duck an insult—he ate there but he wouldn't live at home. He was part the kind of dog in the picture on her Victrola, which she supposed was where he got his name. But most of him was something else. Ordinarily that wouldn't matter, a dog could be ten dogs if he liked, but Victor was two or three dogs right in his face. The upper part of his face was a different dog than the lower, and stopped right where he was something like a Boston bull. But the lower jaw extended beyond it an inch or so. Nearly all of his teeth were out in front of his face. How he chewed anything she didn't know, or even lapped it for that matter, but he was husky enough and always looked well fed. After the first shock of recognition Miss Newcomb always patted him, then Victor would follow her to the corner of Ramona and Yale. There he would sit in a cactus garden until she came back. Miss Newcomb had spoken to Mrs. Bagley about him and Mrs. Bagley said he was normal enough. The only thing she couldn't stand was his shameful seasonal behavior, when he would follow anything, just *anything* in town: Great Danes, lap dogs, fixed dogs, anything. This had led Mrs. Bagley to state, publicly, on several occasions, that a dog like that was no dog of hers. But whenever supper came around there he was.

She left him sniffing some cactus plants and now was free

to cross the street. As she entered the Market Basket, what did she do but walk right into Mr. Bloom, who had just bought meat of some kind.

"Well, well, Miss Newcomb," he boomed, "how you find the bed—is it all right?"

As Miss Newcomb turned and hurried toward the grapefruit, Mr. Bloom said, "I been wonderin' since then why he liked to sleep down so low. Maybe it's cooler down there. Haven't you ever noticed it's cooler on the floor?"

Miss Newcomb didn't seem to understand what he was talking about.

"Well," he said, "come summer you try it. I'm thinkin' of tryin' it myself. Anything you catch Mr. Ward doin' has a pretty smart point."

Miss Newcomb let Mr. Bloom pay for her grapefruit, although she really didn't need grapefruit at all.

"Well, see you soon," he said. "I want to get another look at them books. I never seen so many *read* books in all my life."

Roger Snead, the vegetable boy, wanted to know whose books was that, and Mr. Bloom went on to explain to him. Miss Newcomb, with her three grapefruit, hurried to the back. There she stood looking at the catsup and trying to remember what she wanted, when a very gentle lady spoke to her.

"Excuse me," she said, "but I just couldn't help hearing."

Miss Newcomb nodded.

"I'm Mrs. Krickbaum and Mr. Ward used to paint for me."

"Well, now—" said Miss Newcomb.

"For a year," said Mrs. Krickbaum, "once a week— I don't get around very well and every Friday he would come and paint for me. The things we used to talk about—" She closed her eyes and very slowly shook her head. "But of course you know what *that* is like."

"Well," Miss Newcomb said, "we——"

"I don't remember a single word—I just remember it was wick-ed—very wick-ed." Mrs. Krickbaum gave her the cutest look that Miss Newcomb thought she had ever seen, a trim little look with a quick glint from her eyes. Miss Newcomb was just on the verge of saying what Mr. Ward had said to her about *Harper's Bazaar*—but she thought better of it. After all, she didn't know Mrs. Krickbaum at all. This thought they both had at the same time, and turned and looked at vinegar with the eyes of specialists. Mrs. Krickbaum shook her head at what she saw. But when she walked away Miss Newcomb called out, quite in spite of herself, "I have my Victory Shopper," and rattled the wheels to call attention to it. "You might as well put your things in if you're going my way."

That would be fine, Mrs. Krickbaum said, except that she was going clear to Princeton and she had read that Miss Newcomb lived on Via Bonita.

Miss Newcomb said that many was the time she walked clear to Princeton just for the walk—so Mrs. Krickbaum put her packages in. Even then the shopper wasn't full but Miss Newcomb couldn't seem to think of anything. And there they were, walking up the street without half the things that they had come down for.

On the corner of Ramona, Victor picked them up. But he was so confused by the direction she was walking that he refused to go any further, and stopped to spatter new grass all over some baby's play pen in the yard. He was still there when Miss Newcomb looked back at him.

[182]

Mrs. Krickbaum lived in a house behind a yard so full of plants that Miss Newcomb had never known the house was there. They stood in the yard and talked about this, and about how extraordinary it was that they had lived in Bel Air for twenty years and never set eyes on each other. Not once. Miss Newcomb said that she was glad to say that something like that had been put an end to, and Mrs. Krickbaum insisted that Miss Newcomb come in. Only for a minute since she knew Miss Newcomb was a busy woman, but there was something that she just had to see. Miss Newcomb stepped in and Mrs. Krickbaum went to take off her hat. Miss Newcomb thought the house a little gloomy, shaded as it was, and with the woodwork dark, but she could see that it had its point in the summertime. Around the stone fireplace were books, which Miss Newcomb thought a good sign, and on the hearth was one of those stones the Indians ground flour in. Over the fireplace was a picture Miss Newcomb could hardly see because of the window reflections in the glass. It was in a very heavy frame painted dark to match the woodwork, and the painting looked pretty dark as well. As she stepped closer to see just what it was, from the dining room Mrs. Krickbaum said, "That's it—that's what I wanted you to see."

Miss Newcomb strained to look at it.

Mrs. Krickbaum walked around lifting blinds, adjusting curtains, until she said, "There now, there now—that's how it looks."

Miss Newcomb had never seen such a mess in her life. She couldn't see very much, but what she could see looked like a sliced kidney, or a lot of Christmas candy with the little pictures inside.

"It's just a reproduction," said Mrs. Krickbaum. "The original is in a museum."

"Hmmmmm—" said Miss Newcomb.

"He said I'd never tire of that," said Mrs. Krickbaum, "and I haven't, I haven't tired at *all*." On the *all* Mrs. Krickbaum's voice cracked a bit. Miss Newcomb decided it did that when she said something and really meant it, so she leaned forward and squinted at the picture once more.

"He said some day I'd crawl right into it."

"He—?" said Miss Newcomb. "You mean?"

"Mr. Ward—he said that I'd crawl right into it—and I have."

At this Miss Newcomb turned to look at her and Mrs. Krickbaum said, "But that takes *time*." On the *time* her voice cracked a bit.

"You should see—" began Miss Newcomb, and stopped to wonder just which one. "You should see one in his room." She said this in such a manner that she seemed to see it— although she still wasn't sure which one it was. But Mrs. Krickbaum looked very much impressed.

"I'd really love to," she said.

"I'll have you over," Miss Newcomb said. "I'll have you over to look at it for I'm living in Mr. Ward's apartment— now." After that she walked over to look at the picture again. Still looking at it she said, "Why don't you come over tomorrow afternoon?"

"Well—why don't I?" Mrs. Krickbaum said.

"And see Cuchulain——"

"Cuchulain?"

"Cuchulain," said Miss Newcomb, "is Mr. Ward's cat."

[184]

When she heard this Mrs. Krickbaum started to laugh. Miss Newcomb always thought it an odd name for a cat but she had never got around to laughing about it—now she saw how really funny it was. There was Mrs. Krickbaum laughing so hard that her eyes were crying and she had to turn away and lean on the fireplace. Miss Newcomb was laughing so hard herself that all she could do was wave good-bye and untangle her Victory Shopper from the screen. And then she was clear to Primavera before she noticed Mrs. Krickbaum's groceries —and remembered Victor, that she had left Victor waiting for her somewhere.

8

It was while she was washing Mr. Ward's things—the tops without the bottoms—that Mr. and Mrs. Spavic moved in. There were just two trunks and some cardboard boxes, and one of the trunks went up in their room and the other they left out in the garage. Mr. Spavic came along to help with the trunks, then he went off in a pair of blue overalls and a red pith helmet. It was all Miss Newcomb could do not to ask him about his pith helmet and how useless it was without an arrangement for leaves. But she suspected Mr. Spavic wouldn't understand very well. It was painted red and made him look like some of the bugs she found on her plants, but there was also something very handsome about it. Mrs. Spavic said that since Sunday morning he had been helping a man with a house—the man was making one house into two but didn't know how. Mr. Spavic had done it with whole blocks of houses. Of making one house into two Mrs. Spavic was proud.

Miss Newcomb said she certainly admired anybody who could retire with two trunks—she hated to think how many trunks it was she had had.

"Ohhhh," said Mrs. Spavic, "some day he turn roun' an go somewhere else. When no more houses here—Gregor retire somewhere else."

Thinking that over, Miss Newcomb hung up some clothes. Seeing what it was Mrs. Spavic said, "Is it not hot?"

"Not mine," smiled Miss Newcomb.

"Is it not hot anyhow?"

"They are Mr. Ward's winter suits," said Miss Newcomb. "Mr. Ward didn't have time to clean up all his things."

"Wart?" said Mrs. Spavic, "Hachee Wart?"

"He's missing now," said Miss Newcomb.

"Ahhhh," said Mrs. Spavic. "It's 'bout time."

Miss Newcomb took the clothespins out of her mouth and slowly turned to look at Mrs. Spavic.

"Mrs. Spavic," she said, "I said Mr. Ward was reported missing. Mr. Ward went to war and now he is missing somewhere."

"It's 'bout time," said Mrs. Spavic, and stood up straighter. "I wouldn't wish any man was missink unless it was Hachee Wart."

Miss Newcomb didn't know what to say. She put the clothespins back in her mouth and looked at Mr. Ward's pajamas. In one of the pockets were bits of wadded Kleenex. She took them out.

"I don't wish it for anypody else. I don't wish him dead—missink iss enough."

Miss Newcomb turned and took the clothespins out of her mouth again.

"Miss Newcomb," said Mrs. Spavic, "you see my poy Peter?"

Miss Newcomb nodded.

"That iss wot Hachee Wart done to Peter—he iss not my poy, he is Hachee Wart's poy."

Miss Newcomb said, "Mrs. Spavic——"

Mrs. Spavic said, "Haf three girls—one poy. How it iss with girls leefs only one poy. Peter was most likely poy—who iss likely when there iss Hachee Wart?" On Mrs. Spavic's red face beads of sweat formed as if from pressure, as if her head, Miss Newcomb thought, were squeezed by something. "On second thought," said Mrs. Spavic, "I wish 'im dead." She left Miss Newcomb standing there and walked through the sun to the back door. "That iss pest news," she said turning, "that iss pest news yet—that iss fine as news I've ever heard."

Under the walnut tree Miss Newcomb had put her beach chair, and now, with the clothespin bag, she dropped into it. Shading her eyes she could see down the driveway, halfway down to where Cuchulain, the latter half of a lizard in his mouth, made his way toward her. Miss Newcomb pushed herself up again and just beat him to the screen.

Up in Mr. Ward's rooms Miss Newcomb did a very strange thing. Over the soft cream-colored curtains she had put up the night before she hung her bathrobe and a dark apron that she had. Then she let herself down in Mr. Ward's chair and tried to think. The room got so warm she had to take the apron off of one window and open the door a little to start a draft. The whistle blew but she still hadn't thought of anything. What it was Mr. Ward had done to Mrs. Spavic's boy she couldn't imagine—but she knew just as well as Mrs. Spavic he had done something. That was what had been wrong with him—nothing really wrong with *him* but something that wasn't him added to what he was. So that he did things a boy like that wouldn't do. Like come right upstairs and sit here reading books. If she were a mother and had a boy acting like that and sometimes worse, she would very likely wish somebody missing too.

There was a noise in the garage and Miss Newcomb went to the top of the stairs. She could see Mrs. Spavic bustling around looking for something.

"Could I help you find something?" Miss Newcomb said.

"Miss Newcomb," said Mrs. Spavic right off, "I'm very ashamed for how I acted."

"Now never you mind," said Miss Newcomb. "If I had a boy who did funny things——"

"That's right out of my mouth," said Mrs. Spavic. "That's just what it iss. No one iss missink—still half no poy anymore."

"I know," said Miss Newcomb, "I know."

"You haf some poy?"

"No—but I can imagine," said Miss Newcomb.

"That's another think," said Mrs. Spavic. "If you haf a poy you don't haf to imagine."

"For your sake," said Miss Newcomb, "I'm glad Mr. Ward is missing."

"I wonder," said Mrs. Spavic. "That's such news that I like to wonder."

"That's the report," said Miss Newcomb.

"That is like what you imagine," said Mrs. Spavic. "Point

iss—my Peter iss the same." Miss Newcomb wasn't sure she understood; she waited and Mrs. Spavic said, "Who iss missink anypody when my Peter iss the same?" Then she left the garage and walked down the driveway to the house.

At eighteen minutes after four Miss Newcomb heard someone walking up the drive, and she picked up the paper and read it until the doorbell rang. From the top of the stairs she saw Mrs. Krickbaum wearing a spring hat and matching gloves, so she called, "Just a minute, please," and came back in to powder her nose. Then she went downstairs and let Mrs. Krickbaum in. At the top of the stairs Mrs. Krickbaum stopped to look at a picture Miss Newcomb hadn't seen, right there on the wall where you couldn't miss it, but she had somehow. It was a very flat drawing of an eagle or some kind of bird.

"Now isn't that stunning?" said Mrs. Krickbaum.

"Isn't it?" said Miss Newcomb and looked at it. For Miss Newcomb's taste it was a little too bright and besides, she had never seen such a bird, but she could see Mrs. Krickbaum was impressed with it.

"I'll bet that's Indian," Mrs. Krickbaum said, her voice creaking on the *In,* then she stopped at the door to the room and sniffed at it. "Did he stop smoking?" she said.

"I just don't know," said Miss Newcomb. She suddenly felt very ignorant and remained outside in the hall.

"No—I don't think I guessed it," Mrs. Krickbaum said. "I don't think I did."

Reassured, Miss Newcomb came in and said, "What didn't you guess—so many books?"

"Oh no, I knew there'd be books," she said, "but I was wrong, I was all wrong on the walls."

"The walls?" said Miss Newcomb.

"I thought he'd have them painted," Mrs. Krickbaum said. "I thought there would be murals or something."

Miss Newcomb had that giddy feeling in her legs and had to sit down. She landed rather hard because she forgot how far it was down, but Mrs. Krickbaum hadn't noticed it. She was looking at something else Miss Newcomb hadn't seen on the wall. "I don't get it," she was saying; "I don't get it, that's all."

Miss Newcomb remembered about the tea. When she looked back in to ask Mrs. Krickbaum if she liked green or black, Mrs. Krickbaum was sitting looking at a book. She had taken her hat off, and her gloves, and she looked so absorbed in what she was seeing that Miss Newcomb couldn't bring herself to say anything. She just stood there holding the tea egg until Mrs. Krickbaum looked up.

"Mrs. Krickbaum—green or black?" she said.

"Green, please."

Walking into the room, Miss Newcomb said, "Mrs. Krickbaum, do you read *Harper's Bazaar?*" Mrs. Krickbaum wasn't so sure that she did. "The only obscene ladies in America," Miss Newcomb said. She remained standing with the tray until she saw that Mrs. Krickbaum was impressed. "Lemon or cream?" she said.

"Lemon," said Mrs. Krickbaum, but a little faintly, so she repeated it.

During the first cup of tea Miss Newcomb was scared to death that Mrs. Krickbaum would ask her why ladies were that way. But Mrs. Krickbaum sipped her tea and looked on the wall at the picture that had morning on one side and evening on the other side of the street.

"It's called JOURNEY'S END," said Miss Newcomb, "but it isn't the one I meant." But Mrs. Krickbaum went right on considering it. Miss Newcomb hadn't thought much about it—but when Mrs. Krickbaum didn't speak up, just sat there looking at it, she felt she had better say something. "I suppose what it means," she said, "is that first you have morning, then you have evening—you're young and then you're old—and when you're old, well, that's the end." She sighed, and turned to look at it. In the light of what she had said the picture had a little more interest, a great deal more now that she thought about it. She was about to explain it further when Mrs. Krickbaum stood up.

"I get it!" she said. "I get it—" and made a little click with her heels. "I get it—but it isn't finished."

"What isn't?" said Miss Newcomb.

"The Journey—" said Mrs. Krickbaum. "The Journey isn't finished." She walked over to it and leaned so close that her nose nearly touched the buildings. "It's wet!" she said. "I can smell it."

"I should think," Miss Newcomb said, "that Mr. Ward ought to know if his picture is finished. If he named it THE JOURNEY'S END, how can it help but be finished?" Mrs. Krickbaum turned and looked at her. "Would he have put it—" said Miss Newcomb, "on the wall if it wasn't finished?"

"It isn't finished," Mrs. Krickbaum said. Her voice cracked on the word isn't so Miss Newcomb knew that she meant it. But what to do? Miss Newcomb stared at her. Had she come all the way over here, right into his rooms, just to insult his paintings?

"You may not know," Miss Newcomb said, folding her arms to keep her hands quiet, "that Mr. Ward's paintings are in the world's greatest museums. Anywhere else you have to pay to look at such paintings."

"It *isn't* finished," Mrs. Krickbaum said. "*Per*-iod!"

Miss Newcomb had never heard the like of it. Her voice cracked on the *isn't* and on the *per*-iod, and her cup rattled all over the saucer. There was nothing to do but stand up and leave the room. Miss Newcomb picked up the tray and walked into the kitchen, but just as she got there she heard Mrs. Krickbaum crossing the room. In a kind of panic she tipped the tray, the pot rolled over on the cups, and the whole awful mess fell on the floor. But before she could even stoop Mrs. Krickbaum was there, looking at her hands to see if she had burned them, and not wearing her hat and gloves at all. She had not really been running off at all. Miss Newcomb knew she was going to cry and stood right there in the kitchen and did, Mrs. Krickbaum standing by holding her hands. She let Mrs. Krickbaum wipe her eyes and her face with her own napkin, and then Mrs. Krickbaum sat her down in her own chair. There she sat while Mrs. Krickbaum cleaned it all up and made more tea.

As she came in with it Mrs. Krickbaum said, "I suppose he told you about our predicament?"

"*Harper's Bazaar?*" said Miss Newcomb.

"The *hu*-man," said Mrs. Krickbaum, "predicament. We're all in it whether we like it or not. Mr. Ward didn't like it, but he was in it, and that's why he isn't here right now."

Mrs. Krickbaum rapped her cup on her saucer to emphasize *right now.*

"The reason he's missing," said Miss Newcomb, "is so he could go on doing what he's doing. It's come to my attention that he sat up here in the dark all the time and did nothing but write. But if that's what he wanted to do, why he's free to do it. And if he wanted to paint, why he's free to do that."

"That's only part of it," said Mrs. Krickbaum. "That's only part of the human predicament."

"If there's one thing I'd say he didn't want I'd say that it was a predicament!" Miss Newcomb said this with more heat than she felt, since she had no idea where it all was leading. Or what, anyhow, was a predicament?

"That *isn't* what he *means,*" Mrs. Krickbaum said. There was that *isn't* again, and Miss Newcomb winced and closed her mouth—tight. "The reason he's missing," went on Mrs. Krickbaum, "is because of the human predicament and the fact that there's places where it isn't human any more. Bad as it is, he said, we had to keep it *hu*—man!" Miss Newcomb was careful not to interrupt. For a moment she felt just the same as she did at the Ladies' Forum and she came very near to putting up her hand, as they were told to do, if they hoped to contribute something. *"That's* why he's missing," Mrs. Krickbaum said, "but if he was here he would say that he wasn't. He would say that just for the reason he wasn't missing at all."

"If he was *here*—" began Miss Newcomb, then saw too late what she had done.

"That *isn't*—" said Mrs. Krickbaum, but didn't go on. Her voice cracked so badly that she could hardly make a sound, just a whispery baby talk like people make for birds. There they were, all over again, and Miss Newcomb leaned to the window and pushed her nose against the screen. "He didn't believe," said Mrs. Krickbaum, hoarsely, "that if you were alive you were ever really missing. He said that anything really alive just went on and on." Hearing this, Miss Newcomb wondered if Mrs. Krickbaum felt all right, if she wasn't a little bit upset herself. "I don't know what he means," Mrs. Krickbaum added, "but that's what he said."

Miss Newcomb knew that she had to say something—but the reason she said what she did was because there was something upset about both of them. If it had been just herself she wouldn't have said it, but since they were both a little silly she said, "Who iss missink anypody when I still haf Missus Krickbaum?" It was just mad, but there it was, and there was Mrs. Krickbaum spilling her tea and choking into her hand because she was giggling so hard.

Miss Newcomb was so flattered that she said it again and Mrs. Krickbaum waved at her to please go away. It was a fine thing, a wonderful feeling, and when Mrs. Krickbaum had nearly recovered Miss Newcomb wanted to do it all over again. There was Mrs. Krickbaum smiling at her, she was even looking a little expectant, so there was nothing to do but say the first thing that came into her head. Raising her arm, and her voice, she said:

> A way of bringing life
> Into the
> Com-mu-ni-ty
> Without marring
> Its byoo-ty.

But that was more than Mrs. Krickbaum could stand. She had to drop right down in her chair and there they were with tears in their eyes, and so sick with laughing they had to hold their stomachs in. The tea got cold but they went on laughing, not very loud but like leaky plumbing, and the room was too small for either of them to get away. They would nearly stop —and then one of them would make *that* sound. There was nothing but to get up and leave the room, put on their things and forget about their faces, and, leaning on each other, make their way downstairs. In the open it was better, and might have been all right except for Mrs. Pomeroy's Boston bull, Patsy, coming down the street with five dogs trailing her. First in line who would it be but Victor, and bringing up the end a Newfoundland named Dolphin. So they had to stand there in broad daylight and hold each other up. And there they were when Gregor Spavic came along.

"Well," he said very loud, "you ladees peek lucky one which go home with Gregor!" and then he opened his mouth to laugh, but there was not a sound. Not a sound came from there, but he made such a din with his lunch pail, slapping it on his thigh, that deaf Judge Ely came out in the street.

In the hubbub Mrs. Krickbaum escaped. But Gregor took Miss Newcomb by the arm, and with all the world to see they walked down Via Bonita toward her house. Miss Newcomb with her wet face and her knees very funny, and Gregor Spavic in his red pith helmet and blue overalls.

9

From the foot of the stairs Peter Spavic asked if he might borrow one of Agee Ward's books.

Miss Newcomb said, "Why, of course."

While he stood looking at them Miss Newcomb went on washing the woodwork, looking at the back of Peter Spavic's trim head. He was a very nice-looking boy. Miss Newcomb thought him a little young to be having a wife and a baby, until she remembered how old he had to be. He and Agee Ward should be about the same. That meant Peter Spavic must be nearly thirty years old and she would have sworn he was more like twenty-three.

"You've got a nice set-up here," he said, "living up here with all of these books to read."

"I don't read much," she said.

"What else have you got to do?" he said, and turned and looked at her. He saw what she was doing so he said, "Don't tell me that you do that all the time?"

"What I do all the time's my own business," she said. She had not meant to answer like that—but neither did she think that it would hurt his feelings. A boy as sassy as that had no business having sensitive feelings. But he was looking at her as if she had walked over and slapped him.

"Holy mackerel!" he said, "don't tell me that I hurt your feelings?"

"All I'm telling you," she said, "is what I do with my time is my own business."

"I didn't mean to say it wasn't," he said.

"I don't know," said Miss Newcomb, "what you meant to say. All I know is what you said."

"I'm very sorry," he said, and he was. It was perfectly plain that he really was. Miss Newcomb was mad at herself for talking to him like that, for it was plain he *was* a sensitive boy.

"I just don't like to read," she said. Peter Spavic didn't answer and she watched him looking at the books. Miss Newcomb wondered how Agee Ward had made him like *that*. What could you do to a boy that made his mother sick, and made him sassy and sensitive at the same time? He took out a lot of books but he didn't read any of them. He just thumbed the pages and then put them back.

"There's just one question," he said, "that I'd like to ask him. I'd like to ask him what good these books do him now." He stepped back from the wall so that he could wave his arm at the books, back and forth, a row at a time. "To hear him talk," he said, "you'd think he really had something here. Well, I'd like to ask him what he thinks of it now."

Miss Newcomb stopped working to see what it was he saw. There was nothing there but books and she wondered why he should change his opinion.

"When he turns up that's what I'm going to tell him—and don't worry but what he's going to turn up."

"He's only missing," said Miss Newcomb, in the way she thought Mrs. Krickbaum might say it.

"Well, it isn't for the first time," said Peter Spavic. "He's been missing off and on ever since I've known him. That's how I know he isn't really missing now." Turning to Miss Newcomb, he said, "If I could just tell you what I knew about him, what kind of a person he really was——"

"He was a nice boy," said Miss Newcomb.

"But if I told you, you wouldn't believe me—so don't think that I'm going to tell you!"

"I don't want to know," said Miss Newcomb.

"Ho-ho!" laughed Peter Spavic. "That's a good one."

Miss Newcomb left him there and went into the kitchen, put her head into the refrigerator. From the kitchen she said, "You like a cool drink?"

"No—haven't time. Have it some other time." He came to the door of the kitchen and said, "No matter what he does there is something missing; he hasn't finished anything yet. Look around—what do you see? I don't need to tell you all I know about him; look at his painting. What do you see?" His voice was so loud that she stepped away from it, walking past him into the front room. "Look at his painting!" he said. "He admitted it himself—he told me himself he couldn't finish the thing! He said he planned to paint on it for the rest of his life." He stopped talking long enough to look at it, then he laughed. "Ho-ho," he said, then suddenly, "That's how I know he isn't really missing—he never finished anything and he won't finish this!"

He was so flushed and excited Miss Newcomb thought he would be sick. He walked across to the books and jerked one out, opened it, and stood fanning his hot face with the pages. He went through it that way two, three times, then he put it back and took another one. "*Trembling of the Veil*," he said, "Ho-ho—I wonder what he thinks of that."

How she happened to think of what she said Miss Newcomb didn't know, maybe the word *veil*, or the word *trembling*, but anyhow she said, "And how is your little boy?"

"My what?" he said, then turning, "My boy—oh, he's really fine." The change in his voice was so abrupt that Miss Newcomb wondered if it was changing, or sometimes did what Mrs. Krickbaum's did. "He's fine," he said, "he's just fine. You never saw such a husky little rascal." When Miss Newcomb stared at him he turned and looked out the window. The sun was there, very bright on his face, and he seemed to be seeing something very lovely—a bird close up, or a butterfly extending its wings. "Miss Newcomb," he said, "you ought to have a little boy. You ought to have a little boy or even a girl. I've only been away about an hour or so but by the time I get back my little boy will be different. Like a shadow," he said, and pointed at the table; "every time you look away you can tell that it's moved."

Miss Newcomb couldn't understand why it was she didn't mind. He said it in the same stubborn way, his head thrust forward and his jaw a little tight, but his voice was coaxing as if he offered something in his hand. Seeing him now she understood what it was Agee Ward saw in Peter—but she still didn't know what Peter saw in Agee Ward.

As if she had said so, he said, "But you know what he told me—you know what he said?" She shook her head. "On the one hand he said, 'Now you've done something'; he wrote me a card saying, 'Now you've done something.' But when I asked him why he didn't *do* something—you know what he said?" Miss Newcomb waited. "He said, 'Do you think that having a boy is the same thing as having *been* one?' That's what he said, that's what he said sitting right there." Peter shook the book he was holding toward the chair near the window. " 'If you've not been a boy,' he said, 'then you do what you can to have one.' That's what he said when he was sitting right there."

Before she knew what this meant Miss Newcomb was sure that Agee Ward had said it. This was the same kind of thing as the lawn bowling sign, *The king is dead,* and the obscene ladies.

"And that," said Peter Spavic, "is what people couldn't stand about him. They couldn't stand to hear stuff like that."

"He told them *that?*" she said.

"I don't know—but they knew that he might. They knew," said Peter, "that he might say anything." Picking up the *Trembling of the Veil* he said, "Well, I got to get back to my little boy." On the stairs he began to whistle and went off whistling down the drive.

10

Friday morning Miss Newcomb remained in bed. It was not very pleasant but she was determined to see it through. Near noon she got up and had her coffee, and then in Mr. Ward's terrycloth eggshell bathrobe she walked down the driveway for the mail. There was a postcard for Agee Ward. On the front of the card was a photograph of a toilet seat propped in the crotch of a tree, and on the limb overhead was a sign she had to squint to read:

> We aim to please.
> U aim too, please.

On the back of the card was the postmark Hawaii, and the message:

Westward the course of Empire makes its way!
                                        Gleeps
                                        Bob

It was a clear, bright spring day, and though it was really none of her business, Miss Newcomb stood in the driveway reading Mr. Ward's mail. Perhaps there was something about this card, or the wisteria which was just now blooming—but whatever it was Miss Newcomb forgot that she had moved. As she had for twenty years, she went down the driveway and turned in at her back door. Only the fact that the screen was latched stopped her there. In the sunny sewing room, facing her, was Gregor Spavic—but this time he stood without the red pith helmet, the blue overalls—without anything. Mrs. Spavic, with pins in her mouth, was measuring him. She stood behind him, the yellow tape wiggling in the blond hairs on his chest, his arms out like a tired chicken's wings. Only then did Miss Newcomb see that Gregor Spavic's eyes were closed. But before she could turn away, before she could escape they opened wide as an owl's and with his mouth he made a face for her. And so she could feel it—nearly smell it—he said, "BOOOOOoooooooooooo."

With the card still in her hand Miss Newcomb stood at the top of the stairs and through the window watched Reverend Bassett point at a bird. Mrs. Bassett was standing like the girl on the wall of Miss Newcomb's bedroom, a scythe in her hand, and listening to the "Song of the Lark." Reverend Bassett was pointing, but Mrs. Bassett's eyes were closed. Her face was empty—like the face of men Miss Newcomb had seen in a barber's chair right after the barber had removed the hot towel. It was like Mrs. Pomeroy's face when she sat in her sun window, napping, the *Ladies' Home Journal* lying face down in her lap. Mrs. Pomeroy simply wasn't there in her face any more. It was just a face—and Miss Newcomb thought that maybe she could do something with it, like with a cookie when she put the raisins on. People had to go out with something— but she sometimes wondered where it was they got it, how it was that they came by the face they had. Where in the world did Reverend Bassett get his? His eyes were open—looking, not at the bird, but at the fingers of his hand which he still held, pointing, over her head. He seemed to be wondering whose hand it was. Drawing it in, he sniffed the fingers, his eyes closed.

Cuchulain, who was inside, wanted out.

When she opened the door he came out in such a hurry he nearly skidded over the stairs. She left him there, his tail crooked, staring below. But no sooner had she closed the door than he wanted in. As she let him in she remembered he had not been fed. Cuchulain liked persimmons, cottage cheese, and olives, but in a very private order, and Miss Newcomb never knew just where to begin. Now she gave him ground horse meat and he slowly backed away. Ten, twelve inches away he did what he could to cover it up, his claws scratching at the linoleum. As he sometimes did this in the garden when he was thinking of something else, Miss Newcomb scooped him up and made for the door. But in the hall she remembered that Mr. Ward had said something about that. He had said that it was Cuchulain's way of turning thumbs down. Sniffing the horse meat, she agreed with him. She was standing there, wondering what to do about it, when she noticed her face in the mirror—was it merely flushed, or was this coloring? With the terrycloth bathrobe she wiped the glass and tried on the hat that was just setting there, one of the two hats she had brought up to live with her. It had a veil with black dots in the netting that from a distance looked like beauty spots. She had forgotten about that hat completely. She had bought it for the Visiting Artists Club the year she had been an assistant hostess and had to wear a hat and white gloves. Everyone had remarked how Latin it made her look. Her skin was a little dark anyhow—her mother always said it was her liver—but whatever it was it had something under that hat. With it on, the white plume straight, she was astonished how nice it looked—she looked—except for Mr. Ward's eggshell terrycloth bathrobe. She took it off and put on the dress that went with the hat. The length was bad but that didn't show—nothing showed but her very fine carriage, which was her father's way of describing a figure like hers.

There she was, eye to eye, when the bell that was right over the mirror rattled and made her jump as if she had been at a keyhole and leave the room. While it was still buzzing she was already out in the hall. At the foot of the stairs, smiling for her, was Gregor Spavic. He was wearing the seersucker suit that Mrs. Spavic refused to iron, with an American Legion poppy in his lapel. A stiff-brimmed straw was tipped to the side and backward, and the stubs of round-trip tickets to Long Beach were still in the band.

"AHHHH," he said, winking at her. "Makink whoooops?"

"Hoops?" said Miss Newcomb.

"Makink whoops," said Gregor, "women—sonk——"

As she stood wondering at him Miss Newcomb noticed her veil, the dots dancing gently before her eyes. She had forgotten, completely forgotten, her hat. So that Gregor would never know she stared at him, a little bluntly, and Gregor's hand smoothed his tie down, tripped his fly.

"I am to ask," said Gregor Spavic, "if you like somethink in big town. Cheese—wine? My poy Peter drivink us to town."

Miss Newcomb said thanks very much but there wasn't a thing.

Mr. Spavic held a match to his cigar. Blowing out smoke, he opened his mouth to think of something else when there was a noise in the garage. And then, right there in the side door, filling it, was Mr. Bloom, his hairy arms propped up on his sides. When he looked up at her Miss Newcomb couldn't help but think of the mirror, for all Mr. Bloom could see of her was the hat. He looked from the hat back to Gregor Spavic who was dusting his cigar, then back at her hat again.

"Getting home late, ain't you?" said Mr. Bloom.

"Nooo," said Gregor, "leavink oily," and slapped Mr. Bloom soundly in the chest. From then on Miss Newcomb didn't hear very much. Every two or three words Gregor would thump Mr. Bloom where he thumped loudest and Mr. Bloom would slap his own thigh. He was wearing his army pants and she could see the dust spark in the hallway, clouds of it every time he cuffed himself. They stopped looking at her and so she started back inside. Then in the room she changed her mind, took her coin purse from the dresser, her sun umbrella, and came out into the hall. Mr. Bloom and Gregor had retired into the garage. In the hot light of the driveway she stopped to raise her umbrella, and at the click it made, Mr. Bloom stopped horse-laughing. As she walked toward the street she heard them move to where they could look at her.

Miss Newcomb had seen women like *that*—but never before had she felt like one, and do what she could she knew her hips were wobbling. They were wobbling all over the place—do what she could. Right where the Carob pods began she felt she would shake right to pieces, wobble till she rattled all over right before those men. Then just nothing at all pulled her together again. Mrs. Spavic's garbage pail was there on the stoop and she picked it up to take it with her, holding it in her free hand on the left side. That was the hand that she pulled her Victory Shopper with. Now that it had something useful to do it quieted down, her hips stopped wobbling, and by the time she reached the street she had control of things. But just to be on the safe side she carried the pail to the next driveway.

At the Bowling Green she had a cool drink of water while she read the lawn bowling sign—but the cold water on an empty stomach made her a little sick. She remembered that she hadn't eaten a bite all day. Thinking of that, she heard Victor following her with his harness dragging, and she stopped long enough to buckle him up. Then together, in the sun, they walked down Princeton toward the Sugar Bowl.

As she entered the Sugar Bowl she stopped to look at the pin-ball machine—something she thought she had outlawed when she signed a petition five years ago. Through the window she could never figure out just how it worked. Bells rang, numbers flashed, and little boys too young to play somehow helped by kicking and pounding on the sides. If there had been such a thing in Chagrin Falls, little Gussie Newcomb would have pinned it, kicked it, pounded it, or whatever you did. She was so sure of this that she pulled a knob which was certainly there to pull on, and without putting her money in it certainly wouldn't work. So she let it snap back and walked away. But to her amazement a bell rang, then another bell, and although none of the lights came on everybody in the Sugar Bowl turned to stare at her.

From behind the counter Mr. Conklin said, "Lady, you can't play it free; it's a nickel." Then he walked to the cash register just to get her one.

Smiling—she insisted it was a mistake. All she came in for was a bite to eat and she had just flipped at it as she was passing.

Mr. Conklin was holding out two nickels for a dime. With everybody listening he said, "Lady—you can't have fun for nothin'. I gotta pay myself—right through the nose," he said. He bounced the nickels on the counter and one of them fell over on her side.

"Young man!" Miss Newcomb heard herself say. "Young man—I am Miss Augusta Newcomb!" and with everybody staring she turned and left the Sugar Bowl. She walked right out into the street where some other smarty stopped to holler at her, but she paid no attention until she heard the screech of the brakes. She was so sure she was hit, and she cared so little about it, that she didn't jump one way or the other; she just stood there. And there she was standing when right in her ear, "My God, dearie, I've been looking for you, but I don't want you dead; I want you alive!" When she stopped goosefleshing, Miss Newcomb turned and looked at Mrs. Briggs. She was not fond of Mrs. Briggs—she would as soon be hit as be called *dearie*—but on the other hand had she said that she was *looking* for her? Evelina Briggs of the Bel Air *Advance* and the Siddons Club of Orange Valley? "Pile in here," said Evelina, and pushed open the door. "Pile in here and just consider yourself kidnaped. We've been holding up the works while I've been looking for you."

Faced with something like that, Miss Newcomb piled in. Evelina turned the car right there in the street, right in front of the Sugar Bowl with Mr. Conklin staring, and then they raced back from where she had come. At every intersection Evelina tooted by hugging the wheel until the horn sounded, and then she hugged it while they bounced on the dips. Miss Newcomb had heard about it, but she had no idea how quick something like that got to be fun. Before they got out of town she had caught the spirit of it and leaned forward ready for the last dip. As they dipped, the horn tooted, and in a strong voice Miss Newcomb said:

"Westward the course of Empire makes its way!"

Evelina Briggs found that so funny that she came within one inch of leaving the road and plowing up her husband's row of avocado trees. She was still laughing when they stopped in the yard and ladies on the porch stood up to wave and held their glasses up in the air. Still kidnaped, Miss Newcomb was led by a private way to Evelina's own bedroom, where she might like to tidy up a bit. Right next to it was the private bath.

As she stood in the bathroom Miss Newcomb could hear the peals of laughter from the porch where Mrs. Briggs explained what a witty lady she was. In the mirror, wet, but still flushed, was her face. When she looked around for a towel there was nothing but real Irish linen napkins with a pretty trim of handmade lace. So she stood at the window while a breeze dried her face. Then she lifted her skirt and wiped her hands carefully on her slip, wadding a corner to dry the damp wrinkles under her eyes. At the door to the porch she was stopped by a shrill chorus of greetings and Evelina Briggs was coming toward her with a tall glass. In the glass ice cubes were floating in amber-colored sparkling water, and Evelina was saying that she hoped one jigger was enough.

Whatever a jigger was Miss Newcomb had no idea, but on an empty stomach she suspected that one was enough. In the dregs of her third glass, right in the midst of whatever she was saying, she knew, *positively,* that one was enough. There was a pause at the moment she *knew* this, and from the corner of her mouth she removed what proved to be a piece of her veil. And from her veil one of those pretty-colored toothpicks that were passed around. Never before had those little black dots in the netting bothered her, but now they were popping like bubbles and seemed to be everywhere. Only by squinting could she look between them at the ladies across the room, and such a silly bunch of faces she had never seen. All of them dancing and bobbing like spots before her eyes. And squinting at them she got a flutter in one eye. Through this she saw the room, and the faces flickering like one of those early movies that always ended all right even though the spokes turned the wrong way. And then, blocking it off, was Evelina with more ice cubes. Miss Newcomb had just time to cover her mouth, that was all. With an effort she didn't understand—for where would she be going?—she got to her feet and led with her hand across the room. All of the ladies put up their own hands and clapped. Her veil clenched between her teeth, she crossed the wide porch to the hallway, and went straight down the hall to the back. There she found the washroom, a sink, and a basket, ready and waiting for her.

And there Evelina Briggs and Gregor Spavic, on tiptoe, came in with the light. She lay in the hamper of fresh washing, her legs spilled over the side, but her veil happily fallen again on her face. Leaving her in the hamper, Gregor Spavic carried her out.

11

A noise of some kind in the other room woke her up. She thought it must be Cuchulain and rolled over to call to him before she remembered where she was. And where she had been came back to her as she stared at the stains on the ceiling—and Gregor Spavic, somewhere, giving her a piece of advice. *Oily to bet, oily to rise, an you nefer meet Gregor Spavic.* Then he had stood there with his mouth open, slapping his side.

She heard the noise again in the room and she rose on her elbow and said, "Kitty-kitty-kitty——"

"It's just me," said Peter Spavic. "Don't bother to get up."

Miss Newcomb didn't. She couldn't. When she could think a little bit she tried to think about being angry—she waited for anger to rise, but she felt the same. She just lay there, an old lady that her neighbor had put to bed.

"Are you asleep, or are you awake?" Peter said. She said nothing and he went on, "I can't get used to him being missing—when I get over here I just naturally walk right in."

Miss Newcomb rose up again to say—to say, something—but he said, "I don't suppose you've heard anything from him?"

"No," she said. "No—" She threw off the quilt that was on her and looked at her messy slept-in clothes. In the window she saw her puffy face and her very frowsy hair. She lay back again and pulled the quilt up to her chin.

"I see—" he said, "you've been looking in his Album."

"Young man," she said, and raised her hand, "young man——"

"You've got my card here in your book," he said. "You're using my card as a bookmark."

"It fell out!" she said. "It kept falling out!"

"I'll put it back in the Album," he said. She heard him get up and walk to the bookcase, run his finger along the books. "Before I put it back—what do *you* think?" he said.

"Young man—" she said hoarsely.

"You're a woman," he said. "Maybe you feel different about it."

"About what?"

"Skinny women."

"I've never given it a thought," she said. "I've never been thin enough to make it my business. But if I was *naturally* skinny and thought that was what he meant——"

"He said a naturally skinny girl had her fat inside her. He thinks these women are skinny inside and out."

"I'm just no judge," she said.

"I didn't have an opinion myself until I was married," he said. "It makes a difference when you're married."

Miss Newcomb closed her eyes—but there were more spots.

She opened them. Whether she suddenly didn't care, forgot herself, or felt a kind of desperation, Miss Newcomb rolled over and got out of bed. Over her linty, wrinkled clothes she put Mr. Ward's eggshell bathrobe and without touching her hair she walked into the front room. Peter Spavic was standing at the window and he turned from it and said, "If I could get over the idea that he's missing I wouldn't be troubling you so much."

This was so sudden Miss Newcomb was taken aback. When she saw in his face *that* was what he had said, and that he meant it, she said, "Trouble? Why, you're no trouble."

"Well—" he said, "I'd probably come around even if I was."

She looked at him and he said:

"If you knew what he was like, and that all this time you didn't know it—if you knew that you would just drop dead!" he said.

"If you want to say *was*, it's your business—but I'm saying *is*," said Miss Newcomb. "And as far as missing is concerned I'm not so sure that he is."

"I suppose you're going to tell me that he's here in these books?" He took several of them from the shelves and held them upside down. He shook them, slapped them, and flipped the pages to make something fall out. "Well—!" he said. "Go on and say it. Go on and tell me that he's here in these books!" She said nothing and he went on, "Why do people say that out of *kindness?* It's a lie! Why do they say it?"

"Because they think it's kind," she said.

That was not the answer he expected, for he stopped, thought about it. "Well—maybe they do," he said.

[211]

"If there's any other kind of kindness I don't know what it is," she said.

Peter Spavic looked out of the window, watching something, then he said, "You know, that's the one thing I always wonder. I always wonder if he was kind." Miss Newcomb started to speak, stopped. "In all the time he knew me he never once asked me about my mother—you would think I didn't have a mother." Then he said, "But I've sure got some little boy!"

"How is he?" she said.

"Miss Newcomb," he said, "you ought to have one." He walked to the door, opened it. "A lady like you is just the kind of person who ought to have one." On the stairs he added, "You've nothing more to do than look after him and yourself." At the bottom of the stairs he said, "Miss Newcomb—?" She came out in the hall and looked at him. "You ever think of adoption? I've been thinking about it and it seems to me that something like that is just made for you. It even has its points—you can take your pick."

Miss Newcomb nodded, then said, "Now you come around at any time."

"With a little boy you don't have much time," he said, "but I'll come around when I can."

Miss Newcomb sat in the chair where Peter Spavic had been sitting and watched the little Pomeroy boy wash his white rats. He dipped them in three different pans, talking to them all the time as to how lucky they were and what a fine sensation it was. Their names were Harpo, Groucho and Marx. When they were dry he put them one at a time in his shirt, and as the last one went in the first one stuck out his nose. He sniffed at the last one's long pink tail. It looked just as if he had one great snake-long rat in his shirt, or a new kind of weasel, or something. Harpo's nose sniffed Groucho's tail till he wiggled it. Turning away, Miss Newcomb decided she would take a walk.

She didn't think very much one way or the other about what she would wear. All she wanted was something for her hair, and when she saw how well his beret fit her she tried on his jacket since it was hanging there. It was a little long in the sleeves, but with so many leather tassels it was just made for a lady—a lady a little bit taller but just about as stout. On the floor of his closet she found some shoes—hoo-rachez, wah-racheez—or whatever they called them, and a pair with green leather laces felt as if they might stay on.

So in the bright spring sunshine Miss Newcomb took a walk. Under a dripping pepper tree, the birds crackling the seeds above her, she stood with her hands out so the shells would drop into them. They fell all around her and dropped like rain in her hair. It may have been she looked expectant—or like Mrs. Bassett looked in her garden—or the girl with the scythe still hushed on the wall of her room. Or it may have been just something she happened to wear. Whatever it was, Judge Ely stopped to gaze at her. He was carrying his net shopping bag with the three kinds of baby food and the soybean crackers that he lived on during the summertime. He wanted to ask, he said, just whom she was conversing with? He said this with the great bellow that kept his friends at a distance once they had known the full draft of his third set of teeth. Miss Newcomb closed her eyes for a moment, then opened them. Something in the way she looked led the Judge to feel that someone stood behind him, and he turned, half-way, to see who it was. Only then did Miss Newcomb notice the decoration he wore. Suspended from the collar of his coat was a plush-covered coat hanger, and from the hanger a lady's faded garter belt. Strangely enough, Miss Newcomb did not seem to find this odd. She remembered, however, that the Judge still lived with his eldest daughter, a maiden lady of sixty-four years. When Judge Ely turned back and asked her again with whom was she speaking, she answered, simply enough, *Birds*. The Judge himself seemed to find this more than adequate. He tipped back to peer into the tree, as a matter of verification, then waved his free arm, bowed, and walked away. The metal clips of the garter belt clicked as they rose and fell.

Miss Newcomb watched him out of sight, then she crossed to the park. The men were putting their lopsided bowls in the bags expressly for that purpose and she liked the sound of the zippers as they closed. The blackbirds were already worming the green. She sat on the bench from where she could look across the green lawn to the clubhouse, and the door where the lawn bowling sign hung. While the men were starting their cars she watched Mr. Bauhaus set the sprinklers, and then, through a veil of mist, she read the words. This time it was even better than before. There was not only mystery, there was music, and she liked it best the way it had happened when Mrs. Krickbaum was listening to her.

> Bringing life into the
> Com-mu-ni-ty
> Without marring
> Its byoo-ty

On his way home from town Gregor Spavic saw her there. She seemed to be napping—except that her legs swung in time as if to some music, and on her face was an expression that he hadn't seen before.

In the evening she sat near the window and ate sardines and crackers and watched Cuchulain try to clean the can. Then she had to put him out because of the way he smelled. No matter how many times he licked it, his nose looked greasy, and his tongue left smelly spots when he licked his fur. She put him out and shooed him down the stairs. It was nice and cool there, with a fine draft from the garage, and like she always did, she lifted her skirts. It was like taking a shower but without all the trouble and the shock a cold shower could sometimes be.

Standing there she heard voices in the yard. There was a pipe smell in the draft and Gregor Spavic was saying something—but without his face she couldn't understand a word. It was loud, full of spaces, and a little bit like gargling. She went downstairs and stood at the screen. It was so dark she could only see his cigar making signs in the air, like a 4th of July sparkler, but already she seemed to understand something. When he took a draw on his cigar his eyes lit up like a pumpkin, and the smoke seemed to drift in and out of them. Before she saw Mr. Bloom she smelled him—but she didn't mind. If it was what they called the smell of a man, she was sure a little soap and water would change it, but for some reason she really didn't mind. When she stepped out in the drive they didn't hear her because she was barefoot, and she was right beside them before they did anything. Gregor stood up and Mr. Bloom took off his hat. She couldn't help thinking that in the daytime neither one of them would have acted like that—it was something the evening had done to them. When Gregor puffed his cigar she saw Mr. Bloom was dressed for Sunday, wearing his blue serge suit, a white shirt, and a tie. But during the evening he had opened his shirt at the collar a bit.

"Gregor was sayin'—" Mr. Bloom said, "when I got here Gregor was sayin' that he thought maybe you were busy readin' somethin'. There's nothin' I like more than people who like to read. Like I told Gregor, I couldn't bring myself to butt in on it."

"Now you needn't of," she said.

"We can go for a ride any time," said Mr. Bloom. "Like I was tellin' Gregor—we could go for a ride most any time."

When it occurred to her what he had said, she was standing looking in the kitchen window—but all she did was go on standing there. There was a time that something like that would have bothered her.

"A fine time for a rite rite now," said Gregor.

"Depends," said Mr. Bloom, "on how you're feelin'. If you just been readin' maybe you feel somethin' else."

"All the same," said Gregor, "a mighty fine nite for a rite."

Miss Newcomb wanted to know what time it was.

"Think it's gettin' on—" Mr. Bloom said.

"Nefer too late for a rite," said Gregor.

"Now if I'd been readin'," said Mr. Bloom, "I wouldn't know."

Miss Newcomb walked out to the street light and looked at

[216]

her feet under the lamplight. Then she came back in and stood at the screen.

"If you men will pardon me," she said, "I think I'd better finish my reading."

Mr. Bloom was on his way to open the door.

"A nite like this mighty fine nite for a rite," said Gregor.

"We can go for a ride any time," said Mr. Bloom. "We can go for a ride maybe tomorrow—or the next day."

Miss Newcomb didn't say yes, and she didn't say no.

"If I was readin'," said Mr. Bloom, "I'd first want to finish what I was readin'. When I was finished readin' I would consider goin' for a ride."

MR. BLOOM'S STORY

ABOUT A QUARTER PAST TEN Monday morning I was on my way north to do a little irrigatin' when I saw her on the corner of Primavera an' Cornell. What caught my eye was what she had hangin' around her neck. One piece was in front and one was behind and I thought it was a newfangled ladies' bandana until I noticed the towel she had under her arm. This time of year anybody with a towel you can take for granted is goin' swimmin' and that's how I knew what it was she had around her neck. It was one of these two-part swimmin' suits some ladies wear.

Naturally, I took it for granted she wanted a ride to the swimmin' pool, but not until we got there did she mention that it was dry. Now I knew that well enough myself but seein' her with that towel made me forget it—but she didn't say a word except to say that the pool was dry. I was on the point of askin' her just where it was she was goin', but for some reason or other I didn't somehow. I figured that before we left town she would say just where it was she was goin'—in an outfit like hers she had to be goin' somewhere. But there we were out of town and she hadn't said anything. I had to say somethin' so I said, Miss Newcomb I wonder if you know that these power lines here go all the way to Boulder Dam. We were just passing under them and she put out her head and said, *I smell water.* Now at this time of the year there's never any water in that canyon, and if there was it would be too cold for a swim. But where I made my mistake was in sayin' so.

I not only smell it, she said, but I hear it—and when I said that was just a breeze she got out of the car and started for it. Now the canyon is half a mile wide here, has been ever since the flood, and when I saw she was serious I had to follow her. You'd never believe how I had to hop to keep up with her. My shoes weren't so good in that sand and every time I stopped to empty them she got so far ahead I had to run to catch up. After more than twenty minutes of that, damned if there wasn't water there. Not much, but it was water and she waded in it. I sat watchin' her and she said—Mr. Bloom, why don't you wade a bit too? Well, my feet were pretty hot so I thought maybe I would. Like a fool kid I waded right in and that water was so cold I thought it was hot—honest to God, I thought it was so hot it was cookin' me. Since it wasn't cookin' her I couldn't jump out, and I'm not so sure I could've jumped anyhow—there wasn't any feelin' below where that water was on my legs. When I finally got out my feet were rusty blue. They looked like angle worms dryin' on the walk. At first they didn't feel so bad, then they prickled all over like they were asleep, then they just burned until they started to itch. All this time she just waded up and down in it lookin' for things.

When my feet stopped itchin' I began to like it there. There was just enough breeze to keep a man cool and I think I felt a little bit like a kid—like a kid feels when he sits there with his bare feet out in front of him. The only trouble was that I was about starved to death. But I liked sittin' there so much I didn't want to say anythin' about leaving since I knew I'd likely never do it again. It's not the kind of thing you ever do by yourself. What I'd do would be to drive up in the car to where I could see this spot from the road and then just sit there and remember it.

Right then she said, I should've thought and put up a good lunch.

Well, I didn't wake up right away—all I did for a while was wish that she had—then it occurred to me that I could go for one. I said, Miss Newcomb, why don't I hustle back to Moore's and have him put one up? Well, she didn't like that, but she could see that there was nothin' else to do. I had a hard time getting my shoes on and it seemed a little far walkin' back to the car, but I made up time all the way comin' down. All I asked Mr. Moore for was a double-size lunch. Sometimes I eat that much myself so he wasn't at all surprised. While I was waiting I had some pie so that I wouldn't be too hungry and inclined to be a hog with the lunch. Then I got in the car and came back up.

Well—I had the feeling before I got there everythin' was going too well, so I didn't let on when I didn't find the spot. I didn't let on for twenty minutes or so. By then it was pretty clear that I was plumb batty or that she'd gone off for a walk somewhere. I was so fuddled I wasn't sure which. I wasn't sure any more where I thought it was I'd left her so all I could do was holler and walk around. I walked around till the calves in my legs were sore. I got so tired and hungry that I didn't think I could reach the road unless I sat down and ate a little first. Without meanin' to I ate nearly all that lunch. I'd brought along a carton of milk, but once I got it over my head for the life of me I couldn't get it down. I was born and raised out here, I lived out here for fifty-two years, but I've never felt so pooped as I did sittin' there. I remember lookin' at my watch, takin' off my hat to put on my face—but I was asleep, I guess, before I put it there.

I don't know how long she was there before I woke up. She was asleep herself, sittin' where the sun fell on her, and I could see her nose was sunburned pretty bad. She'd eaten what was left of the lunch and picked up the paper I'd left scattered, puttin' it back in the box the lunch came in. I couldn't make up my mind whether to wake her up or not. For all I knew she needed the sleep, and yet if I didn't wake her up she was liable to think I was worse than I was. Before I made up my mind she woke up by herself. She caught me with my eyes open so I couldn't play possum and there was nothing to do but just look back at her. Her legs were stretched out in front and clear to the knee she was tanned as a berry, just a little white fuzz blowin' on them. She's a dark-skinned girl, Gussie, and I could believe that all right, but I couldn't believe the bottom of her feet. They were cut and crosscut like the top of a chopping block, and some of the cuts were caked up with sand. It made mine hurt just to sit and look at them. I figured she'd done most of that just walkin' around lookin' for me and I was so ashamed of myself I was nearly sick. I couldn't think of a thing to say, I don't know as I could think of it now—when she said, Mr. Bloom, when was it we had the flood through here?

Five, I said. Five-six years ago.

Followin' that up I said—before that this canyon was narrow, there wasn't any of these big boulders you see around here. The way she looked around I could see that she hadn't said that just to start me talkin'—a woman with a mind like hers just naturally wanted to know.

The force of water, I said, is somethin' you'd never believe. There it is, I said, tricklin' in the sand—but you get enough of it all goin' one way and there ain't anything between hell and more water that'll slow it down again. You remember what it did clear down in Bel Air? I said. And she said that she did. Well, I said, up here, right where we're sittin' it was rollin' them house-size boulders like marbles and up a few miles it just snapped off the top of trees. Trees two, three feet thick— snapped 'em like celery.

That, she said, was what I'd always wanted to see.

Well, I said, you can't see it now—maybe after this war I'll take you up an show you.

I just seen it, she said, but I'd like to see it once more.

Man or boy, if I'd heard that from anybody else I'd of died laughin'—but I didn't laugh. I'm pretty sure I didn't so much as smile. She just sat there lookin up the canyon and I knew I'd heard the Gospel truth—and the truth was I'd never seen one of those trees myself. I wanted bad to see one but I was still waitin' for the new road.

Is it much of a walk? I said.

But I don't think that she heard me. It may have been I didn't speak up quite as plain as I'm apt to anyhow; I could see she was thinkin' of somethin' else.

Do they swim in Puddingstone? she said.

[222]

Aside from the fact that the last thing I wanted to do was go swimmin', Puddingstone was ten miles to an ten miles back. First of all, I didn't have the gas—second, I don't think they let you swim there—but I'd seen enough to know better than say somethin' like that. Somethin' like that would be just why she'd walk there to swim. Miss Newcomb, I said, the Army and Navy have taken it over for somethin' private, and they shoot anybody who so much as takes a peek. Not since I was a kid have I fibbed like that and it made me even more ashamed than I was. Here I was a hardy man, a minin' engineer, donkey trips to the Rockies, and a gray-haired, barefoot woman was puttin' me to shame. I tried to look at her in a way that let her know how I was feelin', but maybe I looked it even worse than I thought. Anyhow, she didn't so much as glance at me. All she did was look for pretty stones and them twisted pieces of wood that the flood had honed smooth as your hand. When she had all she could carry she started back.

When I got myself up I could hardly walk—if it wasn't for her I'd still be out there—but I had to follow her back to the car. And the first thing I did in the shade was start to sneeze. I never felt such a fool in my life as when I found I couldn't stop it and she took off her leather jacket an put it on me. It wouldn't go all the way around so she had to hold it on my shoulders until we began to coast and got back in the sun. All that time she didn't say anything. There was so much she might have said I was pretty near sick with it, and I think it would have helped if she'd said somethin'. I had to say somethin' so I said—Well, I can just bet you're plenty hungry so first thing we do is get you home—which is the way I'm liable to talk when I'm a little upset.

She said, thanks very much, but would I please drop her off at the Bowlin' Green. Naturally, I said I would and I said while I was at it I might as well drop her pretty stones an things at the house. I don't know whether she heard that or not for the next thing she said was —*Mr. Bloom, I'm thinking of bobbing my hair.* Now your guess is as good as mine where she ever got an idea like that, but I was so stumped an worried I couldn't speak. About the first thing I remarked about Miss Newcomb was her fine head of hair, which is a sight you don't see so often nowadays. But there we were at the Bowlin' Green and there was nothin' I could do but let her out, sayin' again that I would take her pretty things home for her. She walked up and set on the bench where she could watch the sprinklers goin' and where the blackbirds were already wormin' the green. From where I was I couldn't see any more than her bare feet. You would think it was just a little kid sittin' there, swingin' 'em.

TUESDAY

Think I'd have gone right by if it hadn't been for that dog. But when I seen the dog I was pretty sure it was her so I slowed up, and it was her all right. When I opened the door she got in but she wanted that dam dog in too, so I got out and made a place for him in back.

Ain't that Mrs. Bagley's cur? I said.

I heard her publicly disavow him, she said.

Well, I said, I didn't think she was half that smart.

Like I said, that's the way I talk when I'm a little upset about something and along with people I don't think it bothers any too much. As a matter of fact I think she sees things pretty well.

[224]

Sometimes that makes me a little bit worse, like it did then, so I said—One thing about that Bagley woman is she has nice hair.

I hadn't noticed, she said.

Nice *long* hair, I said, and as little sense as she's got, I think she still has enough not to cut it off.

If I had a bird's nest like that I'd shave my head, she said.

Take my word for it, I said, a bald-headed woman is worse than pink eye. And without any hair you wouldn't be no exception, I said. Now that was more than I meant to say but as sure as you let yourself get to talkin' somethin' slips out that you're in no honest position to deny. I guess I was just so upset by the idea of her bobbin' her hair that I more or less said anything that come into my head. Ordinarily I drive around town automatic—without thinkin' about it I know my way home—but when I woke up we were on our way to San Berdoo. I'd meant to drop that dam dog at my house and ask her if she wouldn't like to step out for supper. Ask her that in such a way she'd think about puttin' some other clothes on—not that I didn't like her as she was but when you step out to supper some of these nicer places wouldn't let her in lookin' like that. But there we were, the whole shootin' match, and I was low on gas. Even if I had the gas I was pretty sure that if I took her home after what I said—she'd most likely stay there. So I just mosied along and tried to think what to do. I was still thinkin' when she said:

Wilbur—where in the world did you get the name Wilbur?

Now I'm known all over town as W. H. Bloom—so far as I can remember nobody's called me Wilbur since I was listed as dead in the first war. I think everybody was so sure I was dead they called me somethin' else.

[225]

That was Granddad's name, I said, but I can tell you that if I ever had a youngster he'd dam well answer to a better name than that.

That's very nice, she said.

Something in the way she said that bothered me but at the same time I saw a sign that said EAT. So to keep from talkin' about it I just pulled up in the yard. This place was made of bamboo with nothing but a straw roof on it that they probably cover with something when it rains. It wasn't a place I would have picked if I could have taken my time about it, since I don't care for names like *Zanzibar*. But on the other hand I figured they'd likely let us both in.

We'll have to leave that dog here, I said, as I think there's a law about it. So she let me put up the windows and leave him there. Ordinarily I don't like a place that's so dark but as I was sayin' it has its points, and a fellow led us over to a corner that was even darker yet. What lights this place did have made everythin' you wore look different, as I could see when Miss Newcomb turned around. She looked about as good as anythin' in that light. As a matter of fact she looked a little better as I couldn't help but notice that a woman at the bar looked sick she was so green. I was a little worried how I looked myself but she didn't say anythin' about it so I suppose I looked about the same. Men don't generally look as bad as women in such a place. I think I sat there four or five minutes before I noticed that a white spot was a waiter standin' there with a napkin on his arm. If it hadn't been for that napkin I wouldn't have seen him yet. When I looked up at him he said—Two dinners? and I said yes—everythin' else just came with it whether you wanted it or not. The way Miss Newcomb just sat there made me realize again what it's like to take a really well-read woman out some place. To show you the way she don't miss a thing——

Mr. Bloom, she said, you just relax and enjoy it. And I suppose that's why it was I thought I might order a little white wine. When I was in France I had some of it—it's not really white, more like the color of water—but all that I remembered was that white was what it was called. They had red wine too and they called that red. Well, he brought this bottle of wine but for some reason he left the cork in it, and without a corkscrew I had quite a time. It ended up with the cork inside—but to show you how she handled that one—all she said was that it was better that way since it couldn't spill. About the time the salad came I could see around a little better, and it was then that she asked me if I had any nickels. Naturally, I just reached in my pants and gave her what loose change I had, thinkin' she likely wanted it for the ladies' room. But she walked right across the room to the bar. Right beside the door they had one of these machines that look like they're making colored soda water, but it usually turns out they're just a phonograph. She put in three nickels and then she came back and sat down.

You like music? I said.

I don't know, she said, that's what I'd like to know.

Now that sounds a little funny until you really think about it, and then you see that she hit it right on the head. The truth was that I really didn't know myself. I don't know as I've ever sat myself right down and listened to it. I was beginnin' to think I did when our nickels were used up and somethin' come on that I didn't like at all. But when it was quiet I said—Miss Newcomb, why don't I get a dollar's worth of nickels and why don't we

[227]

right here and now settle this thing? I don't know whether I like it or not either, I said. If you think it's worth a dollar, I said, why don't we try it out?

She said she thought it ought to be worth that much, so I got twenty nickels at the bar. On the front of the machine it said, *Put in one to twenty nickels*—and since I had twenty nickels I figured we could play the works. So I put them in and pushed on everythin'. Then I bought a package of potato chips and came back and sat down.

I think I can honestly say I sat there and listened to two or three. I think it was the second one I liked and I wanted to play it over—but the dam machine had to go on and play all the rest of them first. I don't know just when it was that I'd had enough. Funny how I'd heard that stuff for years and it never once bothered me, but since I'd been sittin' there listenin' to it I'd thought I'd go nuts. All our food was sittin' on the table but I couldn't eat a bite until that dam noise had stopped. On the other hand I couldn't let Miss Newcomb see how it was. I asked if she please wouldn't excuse me while I went and washed my hands since I couldn't stand all the salt there was from the potato chips. On my way to the washroom I saw there was still a pile of records to play. I went to the washroom and washed my hands, then I washed my face, thinking I'd feel better, and stood around till my face dried in the transom draft. I thought I'd been there a long time but when I came upstairs I could still hear it so I went right through a door at the end of the bar. Bygod it was like sneakin' out of a movie through one of them doors at the side and findin' yourself all alone under the night. I don't think I ever felt better in my life. It was lighter out there than it was inside and though I could still hear somethin' it wasn't so bad comin' through all that bamboo. If I hadn't been sure Miss Newcomb liked music I would have gone back and got her—but though I don't listen myself I like people who do. Then again I thought with that music goin' she wouldn't miss me bein' away for a little longer than a man usually is. I keep cigars on hand in the car just in case of somethin' like that, so I wandered over to the car to pick one up.

I'd opened the door before I saw them there. Maybe I should say heard—since I didn't look until I heard that dam dog in the back chewin' on somethin'. Then I looked and there they were, sittin' there. She had a napkin in her lap with her half chicken in it and the dog was busy on the leg. They both gave me such a start I couldn't have said much anyhow, so I waited for her to say somethin'.

Wilbur, she said, we've come off without feedin' Cuchulain.

Now the one thing I can't stand is the name Wilbur—to lose that name I'd go through another war. Miss Newcomb, I said, I'd like to ask you a favor—I don't care what you call me just so it isn't Wilbur.

How's Agee? she said.

Well—I said—but ain't he just *missin'*?

Not any more, she said.

Now I don't care who you are, a woman like that is pretty hard to handle. Miss Newcomb, I said if you want to call me Agee it's all right with me, if you think it's all right with him.

He wouldn't like it at all, she said, if he saw how you treated cats.

Now I've got as nice a bunch of cats as you ever seen, slick, healthy-lookin' cats, but I could see there was no use talkin' about it. All I could do would be to show her my cats, let her see for herself.

Miss Newcomb, I said, I'll go get my chicken and we'll take it along to Cuchulain.

It isn't chicken, she said, it's duck. I couldn't say for sure he'd like duck.

Now you have to draw the line with a woman somewhere, but with some women it's harder than others. Before I could draw it she brought those cats up again.

Miss Newcomb, I said, I've as fine a bunch of cats as you'll find anywhere in the valley, and when I say that I'm includin' Cuchulain as well.

That held her long enough for me to get away and go after my duck. I told the waiter that my lady friend had taken sick. I'd never fibbed like that before and it was surprisin' how easy I did it, and while he was gone for my change I slipped the wine up my sleeve. That bill was $12.85, which is too dam much for dog and cat food, but I can't say I minded payin' it so much. I left thirty-five cents on the table for him to boot. When I came out she and the dog had moved up front again and I gave her the bottle of wine to hold. It was such a nice night for a ride that I didn't mind the smell of that dog or the noise he made tryin' to lick what he couldn't reach.

Miss Newcomb, I said, I want you to have a good look at my cats. I'm goin' to turn up here and take you by the ranch to look at my cats. She didn't say anything to that so we went north to Baseline and then mosied west to my ranch. Just as I turned in the yard I said—Now you take a good look at my cats. After that, I said, consider yourself free to say anything.

I'd no more than closed my mouth before I saw a cat right there in the drive. There he was, right in the lights, and of all the dam cats I've got on the place you won't believe it but that dam cat wasn't one of mine. Maybe I've got two dozen cats or more, but this was a mangy Maltese tom that spends a little time on my ranch four or five times a year. Without doubt, he's the damnedest-lookin' cat I've ever seen. One ear lies right smack flat on his head and there's bald spots the size of a dollar just about any place you put your hand on him. Think he's Albrecht's cat—the one they call Moby Dick.

Well, when I saw it was Moby Dick I just sat there in the car while she got out and said kitty-kitty-kitty to him. And you'd think he was her cat to see the way he put up his tail and came meowin' and sidlin' up to her. I can't tell you what just one flat ear does to a cat. She held him right there in the light and counted all the bare spots on him, includin' a couple I hadn't noticed myself. All this time her dog Victor was raisin' hell in the front of the car and other dogs began to bark all over town. I felt so sick that when she brought him back for me to look at I didn't even say he wasn't my cat.

He's wonderful, she said. What's his name?

I stirred myself enough to say, Moby Dick.

And what's that? she said.

That's his name, I said, and that's all I know about it.

Well, I want him, she said.

Miss Newcomb, I said, I've been waitin' to say that Moby Dick ain't even my cat!

I want him anyhow, she said.

Now I guess the whole day had been a little bit too much for me, takin' in what happened the day before, and then there was still the idea that she might cut her hair. Whatever it was it was too much for me and I let down the window and looked at her.

Gussie—I said, put down that dam cat!

I don't know whether it was how I put it, or just the fact of my callin' her Gussie—but she put that dam cat back on the ground.

Another thing, I said, put that dam dog in the back!

As I say, I don't know what it was, but she came around and pushed that mutt into the rear. Then she sat down just as quiet as you please and I backed out to the road. And when I shifted into high there was her hand, and she didn't move it, just left it there restin' easy against mine. The next thing I knew we were out of gas but as luck would have it we were north of town and all we had to do was coast back in. As we were crossin' Foothill she said:

It's also a good name for a boy——

What? I said.

Agee, she said.

I like it fine, I said. As a matter of fact I liked it even before I knew whose name it was.

Agee Bloom—she said. It would even do for a girl.

Now I'd never in my life ever thought of somethin' like that. It takes a woman like Gussie to think of somethin' like that even though you couldn't be too sure just what she had in mind.

MRS. BLOOM

WHEN PETER SPAVIC CAME INTO
the room he took the bathrobe down from the window before
he noticed that Miss Newcomb was sitting there. She was just
sitting there in the dark looking at him.

"Who do you think you are," he said, "Agee Ward? I used to
find him sitting in the dark too." She didn't say anything and
Peter put his book back on the shelf. He began to look at some
others and as his thumb fanned the leaves his sandy hair lifted
from his face. Without looking at her he said, "What are you all
dolled up for?" Then he smiled like he did with the jokes he
kept to himself.

There was no reason to answer him. There was no need—
except for the fact that she had told no one and she wondered
how it sounded when said aloud.

"I'm getting married," she said, and it sounded all right.

Peter turned from the books and looked at her. She could not tell from his face whether he had understood her. He did not look surprised; he did not look much of anything.

"I didn't mean," he said, "to rush you into anything. I really meant what I said about an adopted one." She looked at him and he said, "But it makes a difference if you're a woman. If I was a woman maybe I would want to make one too."

Whenever things reached such a pass there was only one thing that she could say. "How is your little boy?" she said.

"I would have brought him by," said Peter, "but he's a little upset with a tooth." He looked around the room. "It's a little small up here too," he said, "and he's getting to be pretty rough. You'd never guess to look at me what a husky little fellow he is."

"Oh, I don't know—" she said, and tipped her head to look up at him.

"He drops back a ways," said Peter. "My father says the early Spavics were big."

"What's his name?" she said.

"We call him Moo-gug——"

"That's his name?"

"No," Peter said, "that's just what we call him." She didn't say anything and he said, "What would you have named him?"

"If he was my boy," said Miss Newcomb, "I don't know but what I would have called him Agee."

"We thought of that—but we picked Ward."

"That's a fine name too," she said.

"I guess I was the closest friend he had, but I don't think I ever called him Agee. It's funny, but I don't know what I called him."

[234]

"They're both fine names," she said. "Ward Spavic—now that's a good name."

"That way you can have one," he said. "We'll never use Agee so you might as well have it." He turned as if to leave, then he came back into the light. "Did we fox him!" he said. "Did we fool him!" Miss Newcomb was not so sure she understood him and she may have looked it. "He thinks he's missing—but boy, did we fox him!" He stood there beside her looking as happy as she had ever seen him, rubbing his hands together and blinking his eyes. "I've wanted to talk about him," he said, "but if you don't know him you can't talk about him. But now there'll be something that we can talk about."

Miss Newcomb looked into the yard where Mrs. Pomeroy stood with her arms folded, staring at the ground. Something was crawling, and Mrs. Pomeroy raised her right heel off the ground, aimed, then dropped two hundred and twenty pounds on it. Removing her heel, she peered down the hole she had made in the yard. Whether because of this, or because she thought of it whenever she was puzzled, Miss Newcomb said, "The king is dead—long live the king!"

"What king?" said Peter.

"Any king," she said. "What does it matter?"

"I never give it much thought," Peter said.

"You're dead and you're not dead," she said, "that's all." She spread out her hands, the palms up, and Peter came closer to look at them. As she looked at his face, she saw that she knew something that he didn't—however much there might be about it that she still didn't know. It was a strange, heady feeling, and she put out her hands as if to continue—but that was all she knew. "You're dead and you're not dead," she

[235]

repeated, and then she remembered something. "Who is missing anybody—" she said, "with Ward Spavic and Agee Bloom?"

Peter did not answer but stood there staring at her. With this power she had to do something so she got up and walked into the bathroom. She turned the water on and just stood there until Peter left. She remained there, waiting, until she heard the loud toot of a horn, and through the bedroom window she looked out on Mr. Bloom's car. In the back seat, barking, was Victor, and in the front seat a man in a palm beach suit that she had to take for granted was Mr. Bloom. She didn't notice the shine on the car, or that the wire wheels were now yellow, but she did hear the motor sputter and see the exhaust. For that reason she forgot the white gloves she had been up half the night to wash, and the patent-leather purse that she had never used. She left them there and ran on the stairs, ran down the drive past Gregor Spavic, past Mrs. Pomeroy with her nose pressed to the screen. She ran because she could not only see but smell that exhaust. And who was it but Mr. Bloom who had said that he had waited all his life for one woman—but what was a woman compared with a tank of rationed gas?

[236]